PROJECT
Conspira

CW00377275

By D

As told by Adam Smith, Cassandra Hera and Claudia Quinta

First edition September 2013

DEDICATION

To the forgotten men of the Apollo program — the command module pilots who stayed in orbit above the Moon while others stepped on the surface. As a result of your heroic courage you helped to expand our horizons in ways that you will never know.

Apollo 11--Michael Collins
Apollo 12--Richard F. Gordon
Apollo 14--Stuart A. Roosa
Apollo 15--Alfred M. Worden
Apollo 16--Thomas "Ken" Mattingly II
Apollo 17-- Ronald E. Evans

They also serve who only stand and wait.

PROJECT BLUE MOON

CONTENTS

PREFACE
PROJECT BLUE MOON

On July 20, 1969 two gallant g men from Earth set their tiny craft down on the surface of the Moon and the world was changed forever. A few hours later on July 21, 1969 the attention of the entire planet Earth was riveted on astronauts Neil Armstrong and Buzz Aldrin as they became the first humans to walk on the moon.

The event was recorded for history as the historical event was transmitted back to Earth via live television feed from the Moon.

When they left the surface of the Moon they left behind a seismograph to measure tremors on the Moon, a mirror to be used to detect the distance to the Moon from the Earth using lasers, and a plaque. The words "We came in peace for all mankind" were inscribed on the tablet to commemorate the event.

Subsequent trips to the Lunar surface were made by Apollo 12, 14, 15, 16, and 17. A scheduled mission by Apollo 13 was scrubbed due to spacecraft systems failure en route to the Moon.

Since that time many rumors have spread regarding the Moon landing. Did the events really occur? Was the landing faked? Was there some sort of conspiracy? If so, why, and how was it done?

My name is Dolon N. Ares. Through years of intense investigation I have uncovered the truth behind the missions to the Moon — the existence of a secret CIA project. This project is in fact the most covert conspiracy of all time — one truly accomplished for all of mankind — code named Project Blue Moon.

The existence of Project Blue Moon has been kept so secret that even some Presidents had no knowledge of it. My informant who worked for the CIA has given me a tremendous amount of insight as to what goes on at the agency and what Project Blue Moon was all about. As the CIA likes to say about these sorts of schemes, "It is so secret — that-- it is a secret that it is secret."

They have sayings like that at the CIA. They like to laugh at the rest of the world because they know things that we don't. They think that people sleep better at night when they don't know everything so they like to keep it that way.

I'm sure you've heard some of the tales about the CIA. Black operations. Secret codes. Covert missions. Conspiracy theories. Some of it is true. Some of it is not. Disinformation is a wonderful tool that can be used to prove or disprove just about anything they choose.

They have people who sit around all day just deciding which information they should allow to be credible and which information they don't want to be believed. It is an awesome display of government efficiency, if there is in fact such a thing.

Most conspiracies have a limited shelf life. The more people who are involved the less likely that things will remain secret. On the other hand think of the NSA phone monitoring that was allegedly done by the U.S. This project went on for years with nary a peep until some private contractor squealed.

That's why they like to keep their conspiracies in house. There is less likely to be a breach of protocol that way.

The Navy likes to say "Loose lips sink ships". Over at the CIA they like to say that "We will neither confirm nor deny the existence of ships, planes, lips, or anything else for that matter."

This brings me to the United States space program. At the CIA they think that the program was the most wonderful thing to ever happen to this great country.

Without all of those satellites that are allegedly up there (which they will neither confirm nor deny the existence of) how would they ever keep track of everything everyone is doing down here?

The space program, and in particular the Apollo Moon landings, are so intertwined with the CIA they might as well change the name of NASA to CIASA. Well at least that is what they say around the office at the CIA.

Yes, I am here to tell you that there was in fact a huge conspiracy with regards to the Apollo 11 Moon landing as well as subsequent Apollo Moon missions.

In truth and fact Apollo 11 was only a tiny part of the biggest conspiracy that has ever been pulled off in the history of mankind. The truth has been hidden from the people of Earth for decades and for the first time ever it will be revealed in this book — for all mankind.

I am sharing this information in order to warn mankind of the hidden dangers that lurk in the universe from forces that are unknown to the multitudes.

If you are paranoid about these things — well you should be. There are times when a little paranoia can be a good thing. I share this information at great personal risk and at great risk of many others.

As far as the authenticity of the landing on the Moon goes let me tell you right here and now that Neil Armstrong and Buzz Aldrin *did* in fact land on the Moon.

This is probably not what you were expecting to read. But then you don't know the full story.

The proof of the authenticity of the landing is regularly displayed to all who care to look.

There are observatories here on Earth using lasers to routinely bounce light beams off of the mirror that was left behind on the Moon by the Apollo 11 astronauts. Scientists use the mirror to monitor and measure the distance between the Moon and the Earth.

Hey, while they were there they took pictures. When they left they brought back souvenirs. Observatories around the world tracked the trajectory as all eyes, ears, and instruments were simultaneously riveted on the mission. What more proof do you need? If that doesn't convince you then nothing will!

Think about it. If the Apollo 11 Moon Landing was such a fake, why would NASA repeat the faked mission five more times? At that point so many people would be involved it would be impossible to keep the secret.

Yet conspiracy theories abound! Of course they do — that is because the conspiracy theories have been propagated by the CIA! They started the theories in order to confuse the public — to make us believe that the landing never occurred.

What NASA and the CIA are hiding is the fact that the landing *did* occur. Their objective is simple — get the population to focus full attention on the "myth" of the Moon landing rather than on the actual event and the historical truth behind it.

What a wonderfully played trick the Moon landing was. In the tradition of the finest magicians who ever lived the largest misdirection act of all time was played out right in front of us — and it fooled the entire planet!

It is a well-known magician's trick — sleight of hand. The magician will get the attention of the audience with one act of showmanship — often involving a beautiful assistant-- and with the other hand--unnoticed by the audience--perform the great feat. Usually audiences are left befuddled and amazed. In this case audiences were left in the dark.

The cover of this book features the *original* mission patch for Apollo 11 which was designed by astronaut Michael Collins. On the patch the eagle holds an olive branch in its teeth as it descends to the surface of the Moon. The patch was never used. The mission patch was changed because authorities in Washington wouldn't approve it!

As Collins himself has said: "It was too hostile, too warlike; it made the eagle appear to be swooping down on the Moon in a very menacing fashion so we had to change it".

The actual patch worn by Apollo 11 astronauts had the eagle delivering an olive branch to the surface of the Moon. A sign of peace-- and of surrender.

Actual Apollo 11 Mission patch

Please note on the patch the shadow that the Moon casts upon the Earth. The shadow blocks out the left side of the Earth. When viewed from the Moon the shadow should correctly be on the lower half of the Earth.

Let me tell you that NASA doesn't *ever* get things like this wrong unless it is on purpose. Well okay at least *almost* never. I'm not counting that Mars mission when they forgot to convert English units of measure to metric ones and the spacecraft crashed.

The patch is an important clue which we will talk about later.

The Earth from the Moon

Who was it that we were trying not to offend with the mission patch of Apollo 11? What secret signal was the mysterious shadow supposed to convey? Who were we trying to tell that we came in peace? Why did NASA make sure that the message was delivered correctly by leaving an engraved plaque behind with the message of peace?

Dear reader here--for the first time ever--you will read the true story behind the trip to the Moon. You will learn what Command Module pilot Michael Collins was doing and why he was doing it while the world was fixated on the first men to set foot on the Moon.

PROLOGUE
PROJECT BLUE MOON

My name is Adam Smith and at one time I was an employee of the CIA. I approached Dolon N. Ares with my incredible story and I found a sympathetic ear. If not for his unwavering investigative skills the full story would never have come out for the world to hear.

Some of you might call me a conspiracy theorist. That was the reason that I originally joined the CIA. I have always been intrigued by the mysteries of the world and I knew that the only way that I would ever get the answers would be to get on the "inside". As far as I knew the only group that really knew the answers to all of the important questions was the CIA.

I'm sure you are familiar with all of the usual conspiracy theories and suspects. What causes global warming? Who shot JFK? What happened at Roswell? Who really built the pyramids? I couldn't wait to join "the firm" so I could put on my black suit and find out the wonderful truth about these and many more secrets of the universe.

Instead when I started my career they put me in a cubicle and I helped to transcribe some stuff from the Library of Congress from Greek to English. What did I transcribe? Who knows? It was all just busy work--all nonsense. Garbage at best. Hey it was all just Greek to me!

Perhaps this is my motivation for sharing this information in this book. Years of waiting for participation in top secret projects while translating Greek can do that to you. At times I thought I would get them for all that mundane work—and Project Blue Moon has presented me with the opportunity.

Yes, I'm a language expert. I even know some Latin. In the interest of full disclosure I have to admit that my name isn't really Adam Smith either. I can't give you my real name but I can tell you that I have written many books regarding conspiracy theories and I have been featured on many television shows on the Discovery Channel as well as on the History Channel.

Nobody over at the CIA ever goes by their real name—it is sort of like becoming Pope—when you join the CIA you select your own name and in this case it is supposed to be non -descript.

To the delight of my supervisor I was originally going to select Joe Smith (a most noble CIA moniker he said!) but since that was already taken (a gazillion times over...) I decided to be daring. They just knew I was going to be trouble when I selected Adam Smith — yes I was a maverick at the CIA if ever there was one!

One day for no reason apparent to me the boss came up to me and asked me if I was interested in a covert mission. I should say it wasn't just the boss who approached me. Actually it was the head of the CIA, my boss, and four, (count them four!) armed agents who approached me at my desk.

Four armed agents was a good sign — normally only two accompanied the director. As for the covert mission--asking a CIA agent if he is interested in a covert mission is like asking a person if more money would be of interest. Of course I was!

After I eagerly agreed I was *ordered* to come with the group. They like to do that because it makes them feel important. As we walked down the corridor to a conference room the CIA director told me that I was perfect choice for the mission.

He told me that the assignment was so incredible that no one would believe me if I ever talked about it—and since I was always talking about conspiracies anyway and no one ever believed me then either—that I would be absolutely perfect for the job.

I wasn't sure if that was a complement or not but I decided to take it as a show of confidence.

As the door swung open to the conference room my expectations were high. I was thinking in terms of seeing the Ark of the Covenant or perhaps the Holy Grail. It never hurts an agent to think big.

Instead at the head of the long conference table sat a rather good looking demure woman. She had blue eyes, curly red hair, and fine features that made her rather attractive, I must say. In fact she was strikingly attractive. CIA agents are trained to observe, so carefully observe her I did.

Regardless of her looks though I have to admit that she was still a disappointment to me. This was my top secret mission? Not at all what I had in mind. That was how I met Cassandra Hera.

She did not stand up to meet me, nor did she offer to shake my hand which I first extended before awkwardly withdrawing it. She looked me up and down as though examining me for suitability.

"Does he meet all of the criteria we gave you? Is he single? Does he have ties?" I thought these rather strange questions upon meeting an individual.

The director assured her that I was unattached and that "He has been fully vetted for the assignment. He is perfect, just what you ordered".

I felt like a hamburger being bagged at McDonalds. She *ordered* me? I thought it must be some kind of personal protection duty. Yawn. I had been trained for far more adventurous duty than guarding a snooty woman. If I was going to protect anyone I would have at least wanted it to be the President. Of course this was still better than a steady diet of Greek translation.

She nodded her head "Yes" in agreement.

The director looked directly at me and handed me a briefcase. This was typical CIA protocol for giving background information to agents when the director didn't have time to do so himself. The case was heavy and I thought-- great—that meant extra time reading tonight.

"Adam, welcome to Project Blue Moon. Congratulations on your promotion. You should know that from this point on you may not share any of this information under penalty of death. The world is depending on you. May God be with you. Don't you dare let us down son."

I didn't think much of the "World is depending on you" line. They give that speech to agents every time. There is no lack of self-importance at the CIA—we always think that everything we do involves the fate of the world. Nothing can ever be shared under the penalty of death. Not even the location of the secret restrooms. Heck, they told me the same thing about that Greek stuff that I was translating.

With that the director and my boss left me with Cassandra and two of the four guards. At the time I thought that perhaps some instructions may have been in order. In retrospect I now know why none were given — there was no possible way to prepare me for what would happen next.

CHAPTER 1
GOLDEN SAILS ACROSS THE SKY

Cassandra stood up and motioned the two guards to follow. We were taken through a maze of hallways to a car at an underground entrance before we drove off towards the Potomac River. Once dockside we boarded a large boat. I could tell it was CIA issued — your typical non-descript craft designed to be invisible by sheer common appearance. We sat in silence as the craft was skippered down the Potomac and out to sea.

I cradled the briefcase on my lap. Cassandra pointed to the briefcase. "You may want to look at that before we get started."

"No need, I'll check it out later". I was young and full of myself. There was no way that I was going to let this lady tell me how to do my job. It couldn't be too much of a challenge guarding one little woman anyway.

"Suit yourself". She turned away and looked out over the water. She seemed enamored with the view as if she had never seen the ocean before.

No further words were said on the trip. It was a lovely evening with barely a chill in the air. Fresh air, the aroma of the open sea, this was the life!

I could have pulled a far worse assignment than this. I knew of some agents who were working on some silly assignment down in Antarctica. Can you believe we had agents freezing down there? *Please*, I thought, send me *anywhere* but *there*!

The sun was setting leaving just a hint of a glimmer on the still waters as the boat engine stopped and we began to slowly drift.

Suddenly the water began to bubble next to the boat and to my surprise what appeared to be a submarine conning tower poked out of the water. Having spent time as a naval aviator before I signed on with the CIA I was no stranger to watercraft though I had never had the privilege of boarding a sub. It was impressive. The CIA does like to make a grand entrance.

I concluded that Cassandra must be some sort of spy and that I was going to accompany her by stealth to a foreign country. Finally a mission worth being assigned to!

A hatch opened and we left our boat to board a small dingy that our escort paddled over to the submarine. Cassandra was greeted with "Welcome back Ambassador Hera". I smiled.

In the employ of the CIA things never are what meets the eye. For the CIA all of the world is an illusion. Nothing is what it appears to be. After a while you get used to it until finally it doesn't bother you anymore. I looked at Cassandra differently. Guarding an ambassador is good work.

Once inside the submarine we were greeted by a man who appeared to be the captain though I did not recognize his unusual insignia. Ambassador Hera spoke.

"This is Ambassador Smith. Take us to the observation deck immediately". I could almost feel my chest puff out. *Ambassador* Smith! What a nice promotion that was. I liked the tone of it— very important sounding and very worthy of myself even if I did say so myself.

With that we were shown down a couple of flights of stairs. We followed a corridor that ended in a room with a beautiful window that featured a most impressive underwater view of the sea. It was breathtaking—I had never before seen such a large observation window before on a Navy ship. We sat down to admire the view.

It wasn't much longer before the captain returned. "Ambassador the sun is down and we are fully loaded. We are ready to get underway."

"Very well, take us home."

The captain disappeared. I waited for the hum of the engines and a feeling of movement. Neither of those things occurred. I did see the water bubbling outside the window and then I could see that the ship had completely broken water. I now had a view of the surface.

I turned to look at Cassandra to ask where we might be going. She spoke before I could.

"Mr. Adams you may want to keep your attention on the view window. I think you may be interested in what it has to offer".

I looked back just in time to catch a brief glimpse of the sea dropping away beneath us in the dark. A submarine that could fly! I didn't really know that we had one of those. I should have known. Of course we did — the CIA has all sorts of stuff that I didn't know about.

In the dark I couldn't tell exactly what was happening. It was silent and the ship felt level as we moved in flight. This was certainly quite a magnificent piece of technology. A short time passed.

I shall never forget the full Moon that night and how it lazily came into view right through that same window. I watched the bright spectacle and forgot for just a moment where I was. It had never looked so full to me before. It seemed like I could reach out and touch the brilliant orb.

It reminded me of a song I had heard that was sung by Judy Collins. I could almost hear her beautiful voice as we floated in the sky.

See her how she flies,
Golden sails across the sky.
She's close enough to touch
But careful if you try
Though she looks as warm as gold.

The Moon's a harsh mistress;
The Moon can be so cold.

My chain of thought was interrupted as I came back to reality. Completely enchanted by the view and perhaps a bit fatigued by the long day it took me a few moments to realize that something very strange and peculiar was happening — the Moon seemed to be getting larger in the window.

I looked over at Cassandra. I started to form a question and she interrupted. "Mr. Smith I think that you may want to keep your attention on the view. I'll answer all of your questions later."

I can't put into words the thoughts that were crossing my mind. It was as though I was in a dream — the Moon seemed to blow up right in front of me. In a matter of minutes it went from being the size of a quarter that I could blot out with my thumbnail to filling the window with the most incredible detail I had ever seen of a celestial body — the Moon — right below us.

I decided that this must be a CIA ploy. They can do that sort of thing to confuse people. The idea is to make you unaware of where you are by feeding you false information in order to disorient you.

Clearly I was going someplace secret and they didn't want me to know where it was. Had I not seen the director I would have thought this a prank played on me by some of the other agents. They did that sort of thing from time to time. If it was a prank it was a good one because the images though the window sure looked authentic.

At one point I could even see the sea of tranquility complete with miniature leftover equipment from the Apollo 11 Moon landing as we passed over it. Then we were taken around to the backside of the Moon. The window showed us descending into a dark crater and down a long shaft.

We approached the crater wall and it seemed to magically dissolve and allow us to pass through it. I smiled. What a magnificent holographic illusion! Finally the movie stopped and we came to a rest. The whole episode was short, sweet and to the point.

"Bravo Ambassador Cassandra that was the best movie presentation that I have ever seen. I have no idea where I am — I applaud you and your team for the outstanding performance. How did you get that kind of detail"? I smiled and beamed my approval towards my travel companion.

"Ambassador Smith, I thank you for your compliment. We did take the scenic route for your benefit. But that was not a movie presentation that you just witnessed. You are in fact on the Moon. Welcome to Danaides III".

CHAPTER 2
LETTERS FROM HOME

I mulled the name in my mind-- Danaides III. I thought that it was a nice name for a secret base. The CIA is always good with code names. Nothing is ever called what it is.

They always have a number too. Danaides III. Immediately you have to wonder where are Danaides I and II? There may not even be a I or II — the idea is to confuse the other side. Heck it confuses our side too.

I started to laugh but her expression stopped me. She was dead serious. Lights came on outside the window. I could see that we were in a huge hanger — the sort one might park a blimp in or some other such huge vehicle. My mouth dropped open. It was one *big* hanger.

"Shall we go visit the base Mr. Smith?"

"Maybe you should call me Adam."

"Very well Mr. Smith I'll call you Adam. Most call me Cassandra."

With the formalities out of the way I was led down a ladder onto the floor of the hanger. I wasn't fooled at all by the ruse. I knew that gravity on the Moon is less than it is on Earth.

It wasn't that long ago that I had seen astronauts Eugene Cernan and Harrison Schmitt on television bouncing around on the lunar surface during the final Apollo mission.

How could I forget Apollo 17 and those famous last words from the Moon? "We leave as we came, and God willing, as we shall return, with peace and hope for all mankind."

I knew my history and I knew the Moon. Gravity was light on the Moon--this gravity felt perfect—Earth like in every respect. They couldn't fool me!

Cassandra seemed to pick up on my thoughts.

"Perhaps you should rest today and tomorrow I can acquaint you with our facility."

I was led to an elevator and we both stepped in. Of all things there was music playing as we started to descend. A secret base with elevator music! This had to be a CIA facility. What will covert operations think of next! I laughed as I recognized the tune.

Once the sun did shine,
Lord, it felt so fine.
The Moon a phantom rose,
Through the mountains and the pines.
And then the darkness fell.

The Moon's a harsh mistress,
It's so hard to love her well.

"You don't like Judy Collins Mr. Smith? She is a favorite of the base commander. This song in particular. She has it played on the base intercom all of the time."

"The base commander likes Judy Collins?"

"Yes Adam, I do, very much." We both laughed.

This was the beginning of what became a very close relationship that developed while I was stationed on Danaides III. Yes, Judy Collins broke the ice between us with one of her songs. *The Moon Is A Harsh Mistress* became our friendship song and it remains so today.

We left the elevator and meandered through a maze of corridors and doorways. As an employee of the CIA I was comfortable with underground facilities — we had so many of them that I had lost count. You've seen one secret tunnel and I'm afraid you've seen them all.

Finally we arrived at my quarters. A very nice suite with "Ambassador Adams" emblazoned on the front entrance. I guess they knew that I was coming.

"Adam, you really should open that briefcase." She giggled like a school girl. "I think it will help you."

With that admonishment she left me alone for the evening inside my room.

It was absolutely impossible to sleep after a day like that so instead I decided to spend the night reading the contents of the briefcase. When I opened it the first thing that met my eye was a letter written by the director of the CIA.

Mr. Smith,

Welcome to Project Blue Moon. Regardless of what you might think let me assure you that you are indeed on the Moon. The facts of how this came to be will soon become apparent.

At the insistence of the Ambassador you will be working alone on this project. Please treat Ambassador Hera with the outmost respect as you will soon discover why you will regret it if you fail to do so. She is far more than she appears to be. Please read the entire contents of this briefcase before you do anything else. We are counting on you.

Best of Luck,

Director of the CIA

Underneath the first letter was a second letter on the official letterhead of the President of the United States.

Mr. Smith,

On behalf of all Americans let me thank you for your service to the United States and to the World. Project Blue Moon is the most important diplomat mission in the history of the world and you should be proud that you have been chosen to represent the world. I am sure that you will make us all proud.

Best Regards,

The President of the United States

CIA agents are required to carry a cell phone equipped with satellite communications and a built in GPS locator. Yes we had cell phones and GPS way before the general public did! Since the phone utilizes satellites for connectivity the phone can be used anywhere on the globe without exception.

The purpose of this equipment is so that our agents are never out of touch with headquarters and are always able to pinpoint their location exactly in the event an emergency extraction is required. In addition an agent can call and receive reinforcements anytime and anyplace if need be.

Still thinking that this might be a hoax played upon me by fellow agents I took out my cell phone and activated the GPS locator. This was the best way to get to the bottom of whatever was going on.

I stared in thoughtful silence at the display as it flashed "No signal--out of service area".

CHAPTER 3
IT RANG LIKE A BELL

Now the mission briefing had my full attention. I continued reading the huge stack of paper that filled the briefcase. While the CIA would later require me to surrender the original documents what follows is my best recollection of the top secret files of Project Blue Moon as they were presented to me on that day.

MISSION BRIEFING

PROJECT BLUE MOON

To quickly bring you up to speed on Project Blue Moon (PBM) here is a summary of the events that transformed the world as we knew it. The details that led to this extraordinary event and the subsequent events are briefed for you after this introduction.

FOR YOUR EYES ONLY

On July 20, 1969 Apollo 11 astronauts landed on the Moon. Hours later on July 21, 1969 Astronauts Neil Armstrong and Buzz Aldrin walked on the surface of the Moon.

Unknown to the world — with all of humanity riveted on the events in the sea of tranquility — while Armstrong and Aldrin were setting foot on the Moon astronaut Michael Collins was experiencing one of the most profound historic events in human history.

Left behind in his command module Collins was orbiting the Moon waiting for the other astronauts to return. On one orbit as the command module came around to the dark side of the Moon and with the other two astronauts on the surface of the Moon the command module was approached by an unidentified flying object which rose up from the surface of the back side of the Moon.

The unidentified craft docked with the command module and what followed was the initial face to face contact in space between mankind and extra-terrestrial beings from the planet Sirius.

During this encounter representatives from Sirius were handed an agreement signed by the President of the United States by which the planet Earth is bound to right up to this very day.

To that point in human history little was known about the Moon. NASA had suspected due to previously obtained information that the Moon was inhabited and was in fact hollow. For this reason one of the experiments left behind on the Moon by Apollo 11 was a seismometer.

It should be noted that when the astronauts returned to the command module the lunar module that they had used to descend to the surface was jettisoned and left to crash into the Moon in order to prove or disprove this theory.

As history records when the craft crashed into the surface of the Moon it "Rang like a bell" for four hours--proving that the Moon was indeed hollow.

Just like the Liberty Bell announced a new era of freedom the sound of the Moon ringing ushered in a new era of space exploration for mankind.

The sequence of events that led to this extraordinary event follow.

End of summary introduction.

Historical content follows in chronological order.

CHAPTER 4
INCIDENT AT ROSWELL

On July 7, 1947 a purported UFO crashed on a ranch near Roswell, New Mexico. The United State Air Force investigated and found that the craft was not one of ours and was of unknown origin.

The pilots of the craft both survived and were taken to nearby Area 51 where they were interviewed by Air Force personnel.

The two pilots were both blond with blue eyes and fair skin. They were unremarkable with the exception of their size, which at five foot two inches each was short though not particularly of note for aircraft pilots. They both spoke fluent English.

They were interviewed separately — we treated them as though they were spies. Based upon the findings at the crash site it was obvious that the craft they arrived in was not one of ours. Given that it was the Cold War Era it was assumed that the craft was a technological leap put together by the Russians.

The story given by each of the pilots matched. They both insisted that they were cargo pilots and that they were not hostile. They both said that their cargo was water. They stated that they crashed as a result of the failure of the craft's magnetic field thrust engine.

Back at the crash site Air Force personnel were salvaging as much of the craft as possible. What remained of the wreckage was scorched from high heat. The conclusion was that the craft had exploded in a high temperature fireball.

Some strange parts and materials were recovered and as a result Air Force Intelligence in Washington was notified. When they arrived and inspected the debris they immediately quarantined the area for security reasons.

Just two days after the crash the pilots mysteriously vanished without a trace. They simply disappeared from their detention cell and were never seen again by base personnel.

The CIA became involved and it didn't take much of an examination by them of the leftover debris from the craft for them to decide that it was "other worldly" in origin. When this became apparent they decided that they could not allow this information to get out to the world — the CIA insisted that the remnants of the ship be examined by the U.S. alone so that its secrets would become ours alone.

By orders of the President of the United States Harry S. Truman the event was covered up by the CIA. As a result of this directive the CIA created alien dummies and planted them in order to be able to ridicule anyone who would later attempt to tell the truth about the event. They made sure that some base personnel saw the fake aliens in order to lend credence to the cover up story.

At this juncture the reader is advised not to confuse Project Blue Moon with Project Blue *Book*. As part of the CIA disinformation campaign Project Blue *Book* was created by the CIA after the Roswell incident to confuse the public and lead them in a direction away from the suspicious activities on the Moon.

The site of the crash was cleaned up with every scrap of material tagged, bagged, and cataloged according to CIA protocol. All of the parts of the aircraft that were salvaged from the wreckage were taken to Wright-Patterson Air Force Base in Ohio for further study.

Over the next few years the debris was backwards engineered by Air Force technicians under the supervision of the CIA. While it was thought that the project would shed light on the mystery at Roswell it only raised more questions.

The craft appeared to be relatively small – certainly not capable of any type of inter-stellar travel. It was too small to carry any substantial form of propulsion fuel that could send it across great distances.

The components were made of unknown materials. Attempts to determine the composition of the materials failed.

While most of the craft had disintegrated beyond the possibility of complete reconstruction of the craft there was a part that was relatively intact. A large tank was recovered from the site. While the tank had been punctured and its contents spilled there was sufficient residue to determine what it had held – simple water.

Not the least of the questions concerned the occupants of the craft. At first officers were confused by the "Aliens". The determination of the purpose of the tank that was recovered confirmed the story that they had provided. On the other hand while their craft was obviously extra-terrestrial the occupants were not — they looked just like any other human beings.

Somewhat paranoid about the strange visitors the CIA ordered government observatories to scan the skies looking for additional craft. It was quickly discovered that telescopes around the globe had previously been searching the stars — and looking right past activity that was occurring much closer to the Earth.

Bit by bit the picture came into view. It seemed that small craft were routinely traversing the distance between the Earth and the Moon at tremendous speeds. In this sense "routinely" meant one or two per month but the activity was sustained. The craft were only visible in Earth orbit and in orbit around the Moon. The activity always took place at night — probably to conceal the movement of the ships.

The CIA identified this as a threat to National Security. The President ordered secret funding and research to determine what the aliens were up to.

CHAPTER 5
GYPSIES IN THE PALACE

By the summer of 1952 an image was starting to come into focus. We realized that there appeared to be an alien base somewhere on the surface of the Moon. Our operatives on Earth had in fact observed ships plunging into the ocean and then rising to the surface before disappearing back into space. We concluded that the alien pilots had told us the truth—that these were cargo ships hauling water to the Moon.

The President didn't like it and wanted to put a stop to it. There was only one problem—we had no capability in space at that time and none of our aircraft on Earth was powerful enough to catch up to the fast moving ships.

By this time UFO sightings were occurring all across the globe. The CIA working in tandem with foreign governments had managed to keep the public in the dark. Disinformation provided by the CIA proved effective as those reporting UFO sightings were commonly being publicly ridiculed.

CIA operatives even donned "Big Foot" costumes to add to the confusion. Soon the public couldn't tell the difference between the "crazies" reporting UFO sightings or the "crazies" reporting Bigfoot sightings. Agents at the bureau laughed hilariously as they spun a public tale that kept the world from seeing the truth.

The President became angry at the aliens and called a high level meeting to discuss putting an end to the "alien invasion" or "AI" as it was code-named.

All of the armed services attended the meeting and all agreed that we were powerless to do anything about the aliens. The room grew quiet before the President spoke.

"Do you gentlemen mean to tell me that the country that dropped a nuclear bomb on Hiroshima just seven years ago is unable to swat a few alien space ships out of the sky?"

Again the room was silent.

"Well then maybe we need to think bigger. Why don't we just drop a nuclear bomb on their base on the Moon and be done with it?"

The officers looked at each other and they all began talking at the same time. Finally it was agreed. We would build a missile--use it to deliver a nuclear weapon to the Moon-- and then detonate the nuclear weapon in order to eradicate the aliens.

At that time we were not sure if the aliens could monitor our discussions or even if we had been infiltrated at the highest level by outside operatives. We received our answer the next day.

On July 19, 1952 a swarm of UFO's appeared in the sky above the White House and the Capitol Dome. As radar confirmed the images jets were scrambled to intercept the intruders.

While attention was focused on the ships above a limousine drove up to the south portico of the White House and an entourage of 10 emerged and entered the White House.

UFOs over the U.S. Capitol

With the limited security of the era focused on the ships above the entourage easily arrived at the oval office and the secretary to the President informed the President that they were waiting to see him. Concerned about the demeanor of the guests the secretary made a phone call that was relayed to all security details in the area with only a brief message.

"There are gypsies in the Palace."

This was code for "Intruders in the White House, imminent threat, respond immediately!"

The President and a few staff members greeted the guests and while the stunning aerial show continued outside the first modern day official meeting between races of different planets occurred in the Oval Office of the White House.

Due to the confusion of the moment no written record was kept of the meeting. By the time security responded the entourage had left the building and only the President and his staff remained. However a CIA briefing file that was later created summarized the events.

The person in charge of the group introduced himself as Dione Perses — esteemed representative of the race of Sirians from the planet Sirius. The amazed President could only listen as he explained that no interference of activities on the Moon would be tolerated and that "Destruction from the sky" would occur should "Any efforts whatsoever be made to approach the Moon."

High level cabinet meetings were held on July 20 as the President refused to yield to the threat. UFO's buzzed the White House again on July 20, 1952. Fighter jets were scrambled but were unable to catch up to the fast moving objects.

The internal discussion ebbed and flowed. First defiance followed by indifference to the aliens who had previously been harmless. As the discussions became less hostile the UFO's stopped appearing in the sky.

The President changed his mind again and held a stormy meeting with the military on July 26, 1952. That evening the UFO's returned over the White House and they appeared again on July 27, 1952.

After this continued impressive show of force the President finally decided to relent and ordered the military to stand down. With that the UFO's disappeared from the skies over Washington DC.

President Truman decided not to run in the election of 1952. The new Eisenhower administration was quietly handed the problem of dealing with the alien situation.

CHAPTER 6
ONLY NIXON CAN GO TO DANAIDES

Newly elected President Dwight Eisenhower had his full attention on ending the war in Korea as well as other international issues. Stealth UFO's and a potential nuclear strike on the Moon were the least of his concerns. Eisenhower had the insight to realize that an unlimited war with aliens in the nuclear age was unthinkable, and that a limited war with powerful other worldly beings was unwinnable.

As a result of his grasp of a potentially dangerous situation Eisenhower assigned the problem to his Vice President—Richard M. Nixon. His instructions were specific—find out what the aliens were doing, obtain an agreement with them, and avoid further conflict of any kind.

Right from the start Vice President Nixon had strange feelings about discussing the aliens with the President in the Oval Office. He repeatedly stated that he had the strange feeling that they were being monitored—that the office was bugged and that someone was listening in on the conversations.

In a brilliant moment of cosmic perception the Vice President entered the Oval Office and speaking loudly and clearly invited "Those who may be listening to meet me at Camp David tomorrow morning for important negotiations."

Sure enough the Nixon team was greeted the next morning at Camp David with the arrival of an alien entourage led by Dione Perses. It was during the series of meetings that followed that were held at Camp David that we learned what the aliens wanted and why they were here.

While Eisenhower threatened China with nuclear attacks in order to obtain peace in Korea, Nixon engaged in a similar tactic with the Sirians.

By 1959 as a result of his brilliant statesmanship Nixon had not only learned the purpose of the aliens but he had also struck an agreement with them. Just as the Roswell pilots had said the Sirians were only interested in our water.

They said that water was a critical component of their propulsion systems — a fuel of sorts. The craft that we were seeing — flying saucers — were in fact transport ships that were siphoning water from the ocean and lifting it into orbit for use by their fleet of ships.

Nixon agreed to allow the Sirians unencumbered siphoning of water as long as the total amount taken did not exceed one fourth of the existing water on Earth. This was considered a huge amount of water that couldn't possibly ever have been taken by the Sirians. Further there were limits on how much could be taken at a time — a maximum of one tanker ship could visit Earth per month.

In exchange the Sirians were to provide access to their technology as well as orbital protection from any potentially dangerous meteorite strike that could threaten the Earth. The Eisenhower White House was thrilled with the deal. They had avoided nuclear war with the aliens and had bought meteor protection and technological leaps at the expense of a few mere buckets of water.

As the election of 1960 approached the carefully worded treaty was presented to Richard Nixon at Camp David by Dione Perses of Sirius for his signature.

While he was engaged in a close fight for the presidency Nixon was confident of his eventual success. Since he was so preoccupied with the election he decided to put off signing the treaty until after his election victory. The treaty signing would be the first act of his new presidency and at the same time it would be his crowning achievement assuring him of an exalted place in history.

One can only imagine the disappointment in the Nixon camp when the election was lost to John Kennedy and the file with all of the background on the UFO encounters including the unsigned treaty was turned over to the new President.

The bad blood between Nixon and Kennedy resulted in a difference of opinion as to how the aliens should be handled. Kennedy felt that Nixon had given away far too much — one quarter of the water on Earth — in exchange for unknown baubles and a promise of protection. He called it "Mobster protection money" and said that "We would bow to no force on Earth or in heaven so help me God."

The treaty was placed — unsigned--in the desk of the President. After much thought Kennedy decided that we needed to meet the aliens on equal ground — in space. As a result his response to the alien threat was to form NASA so that Earth would have a stake in the heavens.

Kennedy declared that he would make sure that the aliens heard our response to their threats. In his famous speech Kennedy shouted our answer from the podium for the whole world as well as those on any other world to hear. In light of this new information — the real purpose of NASA-- you can read the speech again today and see the obvious hidden messages contained therein.

We set sail on this new sea because there is new knowledge to be gained, and new rights to be won, and they must be won and used for the progress of all people. For space science, like nuclear science and all technology, has no conscience of its own. Whether it will become a force for good or ill depends on man, and only if the United States occupies a position of pre-eminence can we help decide whether this new ocean will be a sea of peace or a new terrifying theater of war. I do not say the we should or will go unprotected against the hostile misuse of space any more than we go unprotected against the hostile use of land or sea, but I do say that space can be explored and mastered without feeding the fires of war, without repeating the mistakes that man has made in extending his writ around this globe of ours.

There is no strife, no prejudice, no national conflict in outer space as yet. Its hazards are hostile to us all. Its conquest deserves the best of all mankind, and its opportunity for peaceful cooperation many never come again. But why, some say, the Moon? Why choose this as our goal? And they may well ask why climb the highest mountain? Why, 35 years ago, fly the Atlantic?

Then as if to slap the aliens in the face, Kennedy boldly continued:

We choose to go to the Moon. We choose to go to the Moon in this decade and do the other things, not because they are easy, but because they are hard, because that goal will serve to organize and measure the best of our energies and skills, because that challenge is one that we are willing to accept, one we are unwilling to postpone, and one which we intend to win, and the others, too.

It is for these reasons that I regard the decision last year to shift our efforts in space from low to high gear as among the most important decisions that will be made during my incumbency in the office of the Presidency.

Notice the words "and do the other things." These words appear to have no meaning in the speech but they were directed specifically at the Sirians. The "other things" were all of the things that the Sirians said not to do—stop them from taking our water and then stomp all over the Moon—simply because they said not to do them!

In true Kennedy fashion we were not just going to meekly approach the Moon when we had been warned away, instead we intended to make a grand entrance!

But if I were to say, my fellow citizens, that we shall send to the Moon, 240,000 miles away from the control station in Houston, a giant rocket more than 300 feet tall, the length of this football field, made of new metal alloys, some of which have not yet been invented, capable of standing heat and stresses several times more than have ever been experienced, fitted together with a precision better than the finest watch, carrying all the equipment needed for propulsion, guidance, control, communications, food and survival, on an untried mission, to an unknown celestial body, and then return it safely to Earth, re-entering the atmosphere at speeds of over 25,000 miles per hour, causing heat about half that of the temperature of the sun--almost as hot as it is here today--and do all this, and do it right, and do it first before this decade is out--then we must be bold.

In the grand finale of the speech with true statesmanship, Kennedy extended an olive branch. Kennedy was not trying to provoke a war. See if you can read the intent.

Many years ago the great British explorer George Mallory, who was to die on Mount Everest, was asked why did he want to climb it. He said, "Because it is there."

President Kennedy did not live to see the day that America stood up to the aliens from Sirius. However the program continued after his untimely death.

CHAPTER 7
LET"S MAKE A DEAL

Fate seemed determined to hand Richard Nixon his opportunity to seal the deal with the Sirians. By the time the Apollo space program advanced to the level of being able to land a man on the Moon Richard Nixon had ascended to the Presidency and once again it was his call to decide what to do with the aliens.

Under the direction of Presidents Kennedy and Johnson NASA had been directed to *conquer* the Moon. Richard Nixon had no such intention.

On the day the Apollo 11 Mission patch developed by Michael Collins was shown to the President he went berserk. Fully aware that the Sirians were probably listening he vehemently shouted that the patch had to be reworked in order to show peaceful intentions. Immediately thereafter he reached into the presidential desk and pulled out the treaty that had been given to him back in 1959 by Dione Perses.

Then by presidential decree the objective of the first Moon landing was changed. We would not *conquer* the Moon we would arrive with the signed treaty in hand and extend the olive branch to the aliens. Peace would reign and the Nixon legacy would be sealed.

So it was that Michael Collins carried the treaty, signed by President Nixon, on the lunar command module during the Apollo 11 mission. His orders were to rendezvous with the Sirians while in orbit around the Moon while the attention of the Earth was focused on Neil Armstrong and Buzz Aldrin.

NASA was not sure what the reception was going to be from the Sirians. We had not spoken to them directly since Camp David in 1959. We had shown hostile intention since that day by routinely scrambling fighter jets while UFO's had continued hovering in the skies all around the globe.

Still believing that the Oval Office was bugged Nixon routinely spoke clearly in the Oval Office about the intentions of Apollo 11 so that the Sirians would not mistake the mission for a hostile act.

To keep the results of the clandestine rendezvous secret the Apollo 11 Mission patch had a covert code built into it. This was necessary because the entire world was monitoring transmissions from Apollo 11. If things went wrong Collins was to alter his mission patch so that NASA would be notified of a mission failure on his next video transmission.

The code for a failed mission was simply to fill in the black Moon shadow that was cast on the Earth with a blue marker so that the Earth appeared whole on the patch. The full Earth would signify the need for the whole world to stand up against the aliens. If Collins left the patch alone then NASA would know that the mission was a success.

July21, 1969 was indeed a historical day for the planet Earth. While astronauts Armstrong and Aldrin frolicked in the lunar sand below, astronaut Michael Collins fulfilled his mission by delivering the signed treaty to the Sirian representatives as scheduled--coming through in private for all mankind.

The CIA however was not content with a signed treaty. There were far too many questions that needed to be answered for them to be satisfied. Over the years suspicion had grown regarding the Moon and its origin.

Specifically the CIA was suspicious of all of those small ships. They were too small to go very far and they kept going around the Moon. Strangely there was no evidence of any base on the Moon. Photographic evidence from Apollo 10, which had come within 8.4 nautical miles of the surface of the Moon, did not reveal a base either on the front or the back of the lunar surface.

This evidence had caused another theory to develop that would explain where the craft were going. This was the thought process that led to the CIA theory that the base the craft were flying to was actually located inside the Moon — that the Moon was hollow and the craft were entering and exiting from an unknown point that was not observable by land based telescope.

To prove the theory the CIA insisted on the incorporation of a seismic device that was left behind on the Moon by Armstrong and Aldrin. The mission was then modified to include a test of the new theory. Originally the lunar module was to be discarded in space but the CIA wanted it crashed into the Moon to test the hollow Moon theory.

As planned when Armstrong and Aldrin left the surface of the moon and returned to the orbiting command module they discarded their lunar landing module by crashing it into the lunar surface. The seismometer worked as planned and recorded the moon "ringing like a bell" for hours after the impact.

Thus it was proved with the "ring of the bell" that the aliens had not disclosed everything about what was going on up in space. Now we understood why they didn't want us going to the Moon — they were protecting their secret base that was hidden inside the moon from our prying eyes.

Richard Nixon didn't like the feeling that he got from this bit of deception. As a result even after the treaty was signed we continued to irritate the Sirians by sending our Apollo missions to the Moon. While we did do some scientific work there the real reason behind the missions was to "tweak the nose" of the aliens. As Nixon put it, "We have to let them know that we need to be reckoned with".

With each and every lunar landing the command module pilots always remained in orbit doing geological surveys of the Moon. The CIA had them searching for a possible secret entrance on the Moon so that we could prove the existence of the hidden alien base.

Each mission ended with our lunar landing equipment being crashed into the moon causing the "bell to ring". It was confirmation of the hollow Moon theory as well as a message to the Sirians that we knew what they were doing.

It was the last Apollo Mission, Apollo 17 when President Nixon sent up another proposal for the aliens. This time command module pilot Robert Evans was to meet with the Sirians and deliver an amendment to the treaty.

As a tribute to the Sirian leader--Apollo Aether--
the Apollo 17 mission patch even included a
traditional Earth depiction of Apollo gazing out
over the galaxy. It was a nice touch that was
insisted upon by the President.

Apollo 17 Mission patch

The amendment was simple enough. We would
cease our manned exploration of the Moon in
exchange for allowing us to send an ambassador
to the Moon to monitor the water shipment quota
and to assure that no miscommunication would
ever occur between our two races.

The agreement was a clever ploy by Richard Nixon. The proposal had a bit of devious intent. In order to be rid of our prying Moon missions the Sirians had to admit the existence of the hidden base and allow us to send a representative to enter it.

Since we hadn't been able to locate the base on our own this was a way of speeding up the process and getting a look at the place at the same time.

To the delight of the President the Sirians bought the package and agreed to the deal. Their only caveat was that they would approve the representative that would be allowed to represent the Earth.

Delighted by the opportunity to get a look inside the secret Moon base we quickly agreed to the small concession. With the agreement in hand Apollo 17 became the final mission to the Moon as the Apollo space program was immediately shut down.

CHAPTER 8
PROJECT BLUE MOON BEGINS

It was shortly thereafter that I was approached to become the first ambassador to the Sirians on the Moon. The Sirians had agreed to the terms and insisted that a representative be immediately chosen and brought to the Moon.

Perhaps they didn't want to give us time to prepare an agent for the task. Or perhaps they just wanted to put a quick end to the Apollo Moon missions. For whatever reason I had been deemed non-threatening enough by the Sirians and so I was to be the first Earthling to set foot inside the secret base hidden in the hollow Moon.

The last page of the dossier implored me to observe and report every piece of information that I could possibly obtain on the strength and disposition of the forces that were housed inside of the Moon. In other words I was to make a threat assessment of enemy forces as a one man reconnaissance mission and report back to the CIA.

That sums up the contents of the briefcase — the sole instructions for one man a long way from home confronted with an unbelievable situation.

I have to admit that when Cassandra tapped on my door the next morning I was still in disbelief about my actual whereabouts. It didn't take long to make a believer out of me.

I spent that first day with Cassandra acting as a tour guide as she leisurely gave me an eyeful of part of the base. I say part of the base because it was apparent almost immediately that the size and scope of what was present inside of the Moon was far too great to see in one day. Frankly one could spend a lifetime there and not see it all.

We spent that day in a seemingly endless maze of corridors moving from one area of the base to another. I spare the details because there are far too many to recount here. A corridor is a corridor — though all were lit with the strangest glowing light that I had ever encountered.

Of great interest was a tour of one of the hanger decks. The scene was reminiscent of my days as a naval aviator stationed on an aircraft carrier. There were rows and rows of saucer shaped black craft all lined up. Some were being serviced while others appeared ready to take flight.

I didn't quite understand the mechanism that was used for the ships to leave the base. There was some sort of dual energy field that separated the saucers in the hanger from the vacuum of space on outside the base.

I did watch a saucer enter the base. It eerily hovered slowly through the first energy field, and then stopped before slowly moving through the second field.

It appeared to be quite magical. I surmised that the energy fields worked as a huge airlock to the outside. I was told that similarly when leaving the base the ships would slowly pass through the energy field before taking to space.

Once inside the saucer moved leisurely and silently before taking its place in the row of saucers.

You and I might call the black ships "Flying Saucers". The Sirians called them "Conveyance Vehicles" or CV's for short. It seems that NASA wasn't the only agency with a lock on acronyms.

When Cassandra noted that there were ten hanger bays in all it sure sounded like an invasion force to me. I asked to see another bay and when we entered it I insisted on a close up look at one of the CV's.

Cassandra graciously complied. If this was indeed an invasion force there was definitely no attempt to hide anything. I even got to sit in a CV and I spent a few hours completely examining the ship and its strange controls.

It featured an interesting array of technology. Many flat panel screens and what appeared to be "touch" activated controls. There were no knobs or switches as one might expect.

I am not an engineer but after close inspection of the ship it was easy to see that these were not assault vehicles. No weaponry was visible.

They were made out of a material that seemed otherworldly. Cassandra called it "Goldenite". This was a lightweight material that seemed as solid as iron when I tapped on the hull of one of the ships. She explained that while the ships appeared black Goldenite was a different color but the black covered it for stealth purposes.

Perhaps the most impressive feature of the base had nothing whatsoever to do with the remarkable Sirian technology that was on display everywhere that met the eye. It was not the "floating golf carts" that moved us down the long corridors or the impressive medical facility I was shown or even those remarkable landing bays containing the CV's.

At the end of the day Cassandra took me to the observation level which was reached after a long elevator ride (Judy Collins again!) where we sat down for a meal after the exciting day of exploration.

It was not the meal that made the impression on me but rather it was the panoramic view. The observation level featured a massive window that was carved into the side of the terraced inner wall of the crater. Cassandra explained that the window was invisible from space as it was shielded by a holographic image. The inviting window gave a breathtaking view of the entrance to the facility.

It was here that I learned that the base entrance was located in what would appear to space observers as a large lunar impact crater located on the far side of the Moon.

I listened intently as Cassandra told me about the entrance. She made a point of telling me Earth names as she described the location. The base is hidden on the far side of the Moon in the southern hemisphere to the west of the crater Gagarin and northwest of the Milne crater.

We refer to this location on Earth as the Tsiolkovskiy crater.

The entrance is disguised to look like part of the Moonscape. It serves as a hidden port for ships to enter and exit while shielded and unobserved from the planet below.

Sirian technicians even laughed when they designed unique floor of the crater which was designed to draw the attention of pilots as a landing beacon—but is easily mistaken for a lava flooded floor with basic satellite reconnaissance. They were sure that the ruse would confuse any prying eyes.

Tsiolkovskiy Crater from orbit

The view from the observation level was absolutely spectacular. The word breathtaking hardly does it justice and would almost be an insult to the awesome vista that proved to me that I really was on the Moon.

While we sat and talked almost as if on cue a CV floated by and disappeared into the canyon just as our food arrived.

Tsiolkovskiy Crater

It was in this location that Cassandra and I spent
many hours over the years as she shared with me
the history of the Moon and the Sirian
civilization.

I have to say that as incredible as Project Blue
Moon might be from the standpoint of the CIA,
when the Sirians shared their side of the story
with me I felt inadequate as a person. I felt as
though I was a member of an underperforming
planet.

I will let Cassandra share with you the origin of the Moon and what brought the Sirians to Earth. Please note that the Sirians are a rather proud and somewhat boastful race so be careful not misconstrue the tone of her discussion.

CHAPTER 9
BUT WHY SOME SAY THE MOON?

My name is Cassandra Hera and I am the base commander of Danaides III which of course you call the Moon. I was born on Sirius — a planet that is in orbit around the binary star system that your people call Sirius.

I want to thank Dolon Ares and Adam Smith for the opportunity to directly communicate with the people of planet Earth. This communication is unprecedented between our peoples and I hope it will serve the purpose intended.

Previously all communication between our races has been private and confidential-- held mostly between our governments at the highest levels. For reasons that will become clear the Sirius people have determined that this arrangement is no longer suitable.

As you will note I do not appear "alien". The people of Sirius look much like the humans of Earth. Generally you are a bit taller due to the slightly lighter gravity on Earth as well as your plentiful essential nutritional availability that promotes the growth that is achieved on Earth by humans.

Our race is much older than yours. While your civilization has developed in tens of thousands of years the Sirius civilization is over 200 million years old. By comparison your people have lived just a blink of our eyes.

You are probably asking yourself why such a mature and obviously advanced civilization would come here to the planet Earth. Then, having come all of this way, why are the Sirians on the Moon? These are both excellent questions and are a compliment to your still developing intelligence that you would make such an inquiry. Please allow me the honor to educate and enlighten you.

Sirius is a most wonderful planet that is graced with abundant resources. We have in fact 10 natural occurring elements that are not found on your world. In addition we have the most wonderful rings around our planet, similar to your Saturn planet body, that provide an abundance of additional material suitable for many purposes.

Over 100 million years ago our scientists began to work with Tetron—an element found in abundance both on Sirius as well as in her beautiful rings. While I am not a scientist I can tell you that Tetron is the essential element that provides energy for our Magnetic Field Thrust engines.

To put the power of Tetron in perspective, a single grain of Tetron properly activated and contained could produce enough energy to power all of your east coast cities for well over 100 years.

I might mention that Tetron is ever so slightly unstable so of course our scientists have devised a way to properly harness the energy using temperature control as well as other full-proof safety measures.

In our spacecraft our Tetron energy generating facilities are easily cooled by using the vacuum of space. When facilities are built on land they are typically constructed deep inside the ground to regulate the temperature of the Tetron reaction.

As every school child on Sirius knows the Magnetic Field Thrust engine is the finest achievement of our race. The engines are made out of Goldenite which is a combination of the element of Gold as well as two other elements that are not found on Earth.

These powerful engines harness the Tetron and provide a force that bends both space and time while simultaneously controlling and harnessing gravity. Since the engines are made out of Goldenite we often refer to the Magnetic Field Thrust engines as Goldenite engines. These terms are interchangeable.

How powerful are the Goldenite engines? The distance from Sirius to the Earth is 8.59 light years. That is to make the trip to Sirius an Earthling would need to travel at the speed of light continuously for over 8 and a half years to traverse the distance.

Should I so choose, using a ship fitted with a Goldenite engine I could leave Danaides III immediately to go to my home on Sirius tonight for dinner, spend the night in my own bed, and then return to Danaides III in time to begin my work there the next morning.

No doubt you cannot comprehend this incredible miracle of our Sirian scientists. No matter, you need only understand that it is true as evidenced by my presence here on Danaides III.

Having discovered the incredible secret of advanced space travel we set out to explore the universe in our Goldenite powered craft. Unfortunately though we were blessed with 10 elements that your planet sorely lacks we were not blessed with an abundance of gold — one of the elements required for both the Goldenite engines as well as for the fabrication of the spacecraft that they propel.

I might incidentally also add that Sirius is not the water world that the Earth is. In fact our limited water resource is a fairly common situation throughout the universe and so the Earth should be proud of her vast water resource. I compliment your planet. What beautiful oceans you have!

For these reasons, much like the motivation for your Columbus, our early exploration was motivated and financed by a search for resources — for raw material — to build our impressive fleet of ships by which we would explore the universe.

It was with great joy that our space explorers located the planet Earth with her abundant resources of both gold and water which were suitable for our needs. At the time the indigenous life forms on Earth were only some pesky creatures that your people call dinosaurs. So it was that our wonderful race came to visit planet Earth to share in the wealth of your resources.

It didn't take long for our brilliant scientists to determine that a mining operation at a distance of 8.5 light years may cause issues of logistical concern. At the time we didn't have a fleet of ships or an abundance of the gold necessary to create them so we needed to devise a plan to successfully appropriate the available material.

With much thought and brilliant intuition the decision was made that a large scale approach would be taken to the project. Why send countless little ships to ferry the gold across the galaxy when we could in fact send one large ship to do the task much quicker?

CHAPTER 10
PROJECT DANAIDES

So it was that Project Danaides began. The idea was simple in principle and brilliant in scope. Sirian technicians would work in orbit high above Sirius to construct a large ship that would haul workers, equipment, and supplies to the work site on planet Earth. The ship would mine the gold and then return fully loaded to Sirius with a supply of gold that would ensure successful spacefaring for Sirians for generations to come.

Much like your own Apollo space program where Apollo 10 was a "dress rehearsal" for the actual Moon landing we took several trial runs demonstrating the capability of the Danaides program before going live with the actual production.

Danaides I was the first demonstration of the practicality of the project. Danaides I was assembled in orbit around Sirius using materials from the rings of Sirius. The materials were fused together using a Tetron energy reaction.

The finished product was a wonderful piece of technical achievement that was 360 feet wide. After the unit cooled down a small Goldenite engine was installed with remote activation capability.

Technicians watched in awed wonder of their splendid achievement as Danaides I left orbit from Sirius and headed out into space. The unit successfully arrived in your galaxy and was remotely put into an orbit consistent with that of Earth.

While some of the surface flaked off during transit most of the unit arrived intact. This successful test proved our ability to construct a unit from Sirius ring materials and to successfully transport it to the work site.

Danaides I still stands as a remarkable achievement of Sirius technology. It currently remains in an orbit around your sun in a path similar to that of the Earth. I believe your astronomical persons have dubbed the craft 2002 AA29 but in fact this is Danaides I.

With the successful test behind them our scientists became bolder. Clearly a larger scale would be needed to complete all mission objectives. Danaides II became the vision of majestic scale that was required.

Danaides II was also built in orbit around Sirius using material from the rings. The massive unit was 3.1 miles across. The Tetron reaction required to fuse the material was set off at the center of the mass. The controlled reaction hollowed out the core of Danaides II and left the disk glowing red in the skies above Sirius for quite some time as the unit cooled down.

Pleased with demonstrating the production process on a larger scale a much bigger Goldenite engine was installed and the ship was remotely sent to your galaxy. The intent was to shadow Danaides I in orbit around your sun but difficulties with the remote process caused by the size of Danaides II caused a malfunction. Instead the unit went into a kind of a horseshoe shaped orbit.

In fact Danaides II does not orbit the Earth — it has an orbit that takes it inside the orbit of your Mercury planet and outside the orbit of your Mars planet. It orbits the sun every Earth year but takes 770 years to actually orbit the Earth.

Your people are aware of Danaides II and in fact call it 3753 Cruithne. It is an odd name you have for such a wonderful accomplishment of ours but you call it that nonetheless.

Our scientists were concerned by the failure of Danaides II to orbit correctly. A greater malfunction may have caused a larger orbiting variance with possible negative consequences.

It was decided that in order to safely preserve the potential mining operation that it would be necessary to have an onboard crew pilot the final ship.

Danaides III was the epitome of Sirius technology that would boast the supremacy of Sirius know-how to the universe for the ages. It was also constructed in high orbit around Sirius. Danaides III is one thousand miles across with a surface area of 14.6 million square miles. It is a remarkable engineering feat unparalleled anywhere in the universe.

When Danaides III was fused it lit the sky up above Sirius for an entire Sirius year while the material cooled. During this period additional material from the rings of Sirius bumped the surface creating the craters that are seen today.

The center was hollow just like Danaides II and was fitted not only with the finest Goldenite engine ever conceived but also with the first landing bay ever constructed specifically for mining operations on another planet.

When Danaides III left Sirius Orbit the core was less than 1% filled leaving plenty of room for mining materials. There were several completed structures installed including crew and office accommodations. A small fleet of cargo ships and excavating ships were in the landing bay. A Tetron powered gravitational unit was installed to provide a gravity field inside of Danaides III that mirrored the gravity of Sirius. Food stores and oxygen generators rounded out the work that was completed here.

Sirians loved the glow of Danaides III in orbit around our planet. Such a beautiful sight it was! History records that citizens were saddened that such a beautiful creation had to leave us but necessity required that it had to be done.

The entire planet of Sirius watched in awe and wonder as Danaides III left orbit on its way to Earth. Scientists here were thrilled as the Goldenite engine and navigational units worked to perfection.

A whole planet waited in anticipation. Finally word was transmitted back to Sirius — Danaides III had arrived in Earth orbit as designed and was ready to become operational. Our planet was proud of the great achievement that was a marvel of engineering acumen on a size and scale never seen before or since anywhere in the universe.

The far side of the Moon as captured by an incoming CV is pictured above.

CHAPTER 11
OCEANUS PRIME

The insertion of Danaides III into Earth orbit caused some minor disturbances down on the surface but none were thought to be of such consequence so as to inhibit mining operations. As the tidal forces settled down the mining teams began to scout for possible locations for the initial operations.

These events occurred some hundreds of thousands of Earth years ago. At that time the planet below Danaides III was not at all like the planet that is seen today. While geological positioning has changed since the early times I can use current points of reference to indicate where operations took place.

Our geologists found four tremendously abundant deposits of Gold which could easily be mined by our excavating ships.

Our four outposts were called: Oceanus Prime, Tethys Mountains, Eurybia Highlands, and Coeus Major.

Our teams were not used to seeing such vast oceans of water so they naturally selected Oceanus Prime as the initial site to mine for gold. The beautiful island was rich in gold and had rivers flowing in every direction across it. Oceanus Prime was not only the first settlement site it was also the largest colony that Sirius ever settled on the Earth.

Of the 10,000 people that had made the trip from Sirius 8,000 were settled on Oceanus Prime. In just a few short years a magnificent city emerged that was so beautiful as to rival any city on Sirius.

At one point visitors were actually coming from Sirius to vacation at Oceanus Prime. Not only did they frolic in water such as had not ever been seen on Sirius but they could take some back home with them. The fluid was so precious back on Sirius that they could sell a few containers and recoup the cost of the trip.

Oceanus Prime remains one of the saddest chapters in the history of Sirius. At the height of the mining operation there and with over 10,000 workers and tourists present on the island a terrible accident occurred at the Tetron energy facility that powered the city.

During a tropical storm a bolt of lightning struck the communications tower of the facility and it disrupted the temperature control system. As a result the Tetron energy field went out of control instantly throwing off an energy burst of immeasurable proportion.

As residents ran screaming for cover some managed to escape to the sea as the energy facility exploded in a plume of heat so intense that it melted the ground that it was built upon.

The subsoil literally disintegrated beneath the city from the energy released. The explosion actually shook Danaides III in orbit and scorched the surface of the side facing the Earth.

They say that part of the surface of Danaides III actually turned to glass but I never believed that tale. It does speak to the power of our Tetron technology that anyone would even suggest it though, don't you think? Tetron *is* rather remarkable!

Onlookers on Danaides III were helpless to assist and could only watch our monitors in horror as Oceanus Prime sunk into the ocean and then disappeared from sight in its entirety with over 10,000 souls lost in just a few moments time. It remains the single largest loss of life in the history of Sirius to this day.

As a result of the incident it was decreed that all Tetron energy facilities, including those on Sirius, were to be moved underground. By burying the facilities deep under the soil the temperature of the reactors could remain constant and they would also be safe from possible storm damage.

In defense of our elite scientists it should be noted that the cloud cover that occurs on Earth is not present on Sirius. It takes a substantial amount of water to cause this floating vapor and of course water is in short supply on Sirius. Such moisture had never been encountered before by our technicians.

The accident left such a scar on the psyche of Sirius that tourists from Sirius never returned to Earth. From that event forward only small groups of junior minors remained doing the excavating work that needed to be done.

The site of Oceanus Prime has no geological equivalent on Earth today. The story does exist in history however as it has been retold over the years and is now known even to Earthlings. On Earth Oceanus Prime is often referred to as the Lost City of Atlantis.

Mining continued at camps located at the Tethys Mountains and at the Eurybia Highlands.

The Tethys Mountains had the most abundant gold deposits so the largest equipment operated there. In just a few decades the 10,000 foot mountain peaks of gold were removed and excavation continued until the gold deposits ran out at a depth of over 1 mile in some places. This gold was removed by cargo ships and hauled into storage in facilities on Danaides III.

The Tethys Mountains were a topic of discussion for years on Sirius. Not just for the tremendous amount of gold that had been removed there but also for aesthetic reasons. Some factions felt that the trench left behind was not visually appealing and advocated some sort of back filling project that would restore the mountain range.

Others thought that the beautiful river that meandered through the bottom of the excavation was sufficiently appealing to leave the site as it was. In the end artistic aspirations lost out to the cost of reclaiming the natural beauty of the site so the site was abandoned and left unrestored. Today the site is known on Earth as the Grand Canyon.

When work was completed at the Tethys Mountains equipment from the site was relocated to Coeus Major. The first step in the relocation was to dig a deep trench that would house the Tetron energy facility that would power the outpost. The shaft was dug deep into the Earth and the unit was installed and made operational just as disaster struck at the Eurybia Highlands.

The Eurybia Highlands were the sister site to the Tethys Mountains. Just like the Tethys range the Eurybia Highlands were a tall mountain range loaded with gold deposits. Miners had scooped out virtually all of the gold and had actually flattened the landscape to the point of beginning excavations.

Though it had been years since the Oceanus Prime incident workers at Eurybia had been too busy with mining operations to relocate their Tetron energy facility underground.

It is believed that a CV pilot returning from Danaides III fell asleep as he was landing his vehicle and as a result the vehicle crashed into the Tetron facility that powered the Eurybia encampment. The resulting explosion was even greater than the explosion at Oceanus Prime though with fewer workers present the loss of life was far less.

Oceanus Prime was surrounded by water that helped to reduce the impact of the malfunction but Eurybia was completely land based. The soil at Eurybia was loose and there were mounds of soil everywhere around the Tetron energy facility from the mining operation when the explosion occurred. The dust that was created billowed up into the atmosphere while the blast created a massive crater in the Earth.

This turned out to be the end of all mining operations on the planet Earth. Sadly it was also a catastrophic blow to the ecology of the planet. Workers were immediately evacuated from Coeus Major for their safety.

With the sun blotted out from the dust in the atmosphere the era you know as the ice age set in on planet Earth. With no further work possible on Earth workers on Danaides III were sent home and the base was abandoned.

Due to the tragedy that surrounded the mining operations the gold that had been brought up from the mining operations was considered "ill-gotten gains" and "bad luck" to possess so it was left behind and remains today in storage deep inside Danaides III.

There is no geological equivalent today for the Eurybia Highlands. The site is marked by what you call the Chicxulub crater just off the Yucatan peninsula in the Gulf of Mexico.

With weather conditions rapidly deteriorating at Coeus Major the workers left in a hurry. Mining was never commenced on the site as workers had only recently arrived and had not yet set up a complete operation.

The newly installed Tetron energy facility which was deep underground was buried by the snow from the Ice Age. Since the facility had not been back-filled from the excavation that occurred during construction the feature still exists today and is known as the Wilkes Land Crater in Antarctica.

CHAPTER 12
CERCOPES AND ARKE

The Sirius era of grand exploration did not end with the misfortunate occurrences on Earth. Accidents do happen and we are not daunted by them. Our resolve overcomes our sadness at times like these and our work always continues.

Sirians have an inner need to quest for knowledge and to explore. Though slowed by a shortage of gold we continued undeterred to build our fleet of ships. As the fleet grew in number we set out to explore the vastness of space.

It took quite some time but eventually our fleet located two other systems that contained life similar to our own. Just as your Columbus bravely discovered the West Indies our intrepid explorers discovered Cercopes and Arke.

We were overjoyed to find other civilizations so close to our home planet and relations began immediately. By the time this occurred the Ice Age on Earth had come to an end.

The people of Cercopes have twin planets in their solar system that support life. While Sirians are peaceful people the Cercopians are war-like people. The two planets of Cercopes have each been fighting for generations with raids between the planets stealing goods a relatively routine occurrence.

You can be certain that wherever there has been mischief or a fight in the universe the Cercopes people have probably played a hand. Their expertise is in inciting wars between others while not directly participating. When the carnage ends and nations have been decimated they move in to loot the remains of the decimated civilization. I think the less said about these people at this time the better.

The people of Arke on the other hand are of high intelligence — almost at the level of Sirians — but with an added touch of a cosmic sense of humor. The Arkians are also spiritual people who speak in a strange language called Latinus which is not widely used.

You can always tell where Arke has been by evidence of their signature language. I will elaborate on these relationships and their relevance to Earth in just a moment but I think that first you should know who you are dealing with when it comes to the people of Arke.

What kind of sense of humor do the Arkians have? Let me demonstrate. When they heard that Earth was sending out probes to Mars they decided it was a great opportunity for setting up a prank. They quickly dispatched a group of artists to Mars well ahead of the launch of your probes and spent solar months applying graffiti to the surface of the planet.

Perhaps you heard the cosmic laughter when your Viking Space Craft transmitted this image from the surface on July 26, 1976.

Face on Mars

The Arkians thought that the prank was hysterical and laughed for months at the reaction that humans had to their work. Adding to the devious joke is that like many of their tricks the image may only be viewed from orbit—when standing on the surface of Mars no image is visible.

They are still snickering today at the efforts of subsequent Mars missions and rumor has it they plan on planting more "evidence" on the surface of Mars soon.

My point is that while Sirians take science very seriously obviously the Arkians don't. Just so you know what you are dealing with there.

Anyway both Cercopes and Arke lie precisely 8.6 light years away from Earth—the same distance as Sirius—only in different directions. If you plotted Sirius and the two other worlds on a map of the stars you would see three equally sized prongs forming a perfectly uniform "Y" shape— with the Earth sitting exactly at the point in the middle where the three prongs meet.

Commerce has developed and is quite common now between these three systems. Travel is routine as the races zip across the divide between us right past the planet Earth.

Sirius, Cercopes, and Arke have many things in common. Not only do we all have the 10 elements that are missing from Earth including Tetron, all three planets are mostly somewhat devoid of one important component of life — water.

As it turns out so is most of the known universe. There are drips and drabs here and there — just enough to barely support life — but not nearly enough to go around for all of us.

So as you can imagine it didn't take much time before travelers began to take notice of the blue planet with the beautiful oceans. To make a long story short, it wasn't long before Sirians returned to Danaides III and the Earth became a routine rest stop for travelers from Sirius, Cercopes, and Arke.

Generally travelers to Earth are only looking for a few things. They all want to scoop up some water to take home with them and of course some of them want fresh fruit and vegetables.

Other than that Earth is of no particular interest since now most of the gold deposits have been removed.

Such wonderful produce your planet has! Your children must joyously consume the beans, peas, and broccoli from the fields! I have to say that those round red tomatoes are worth the trip from Sirius all by themselves!

Everyone understands that these operations must remain covert—they are sure that Earth inhabitants would never knowingly share such a rare and precious commodity. So "the goods" are all confiscated under the cover of darkness so that hopefully nobody will notice.

There is one caveat here—as you might expect the Arkians can't resist a good prank. So if you ever have wondered what the origin of "crop circles" was—well just think of an Arkian stopping for fresh vegetables and you have the mystery solved. They take the goods and leave behind some of their graffiti. I can hear them snickering even now!

Crop Circle

CHAPTER 13
EX LUNA, SCIENTIA
(From the Moon, Knowledge)

Now that you have an idea of the background of the situation you can begin to understand more current events.

After Adam was brought to Danaides III I shared much of Sirian history with Adam which I know that he dutifully reported to the CIA. Adam correctly conveyed that we were transporting and shipping water to other places from Danaides III and that there was no threat to Earth.

How benign is the Sirian threat to Earth? Well, you know those ships that buzzed the White House back in 1952? Those were specially trained pilots flying their CVs. They had to be trained because we needed to put on a show for the White House.

Our aviators normally transport cargo in their CVs and as such have no background as assault pilots. So they had to be shown how to fly in a "threatening" manner. Then they kept their landing lights on so that they would be visible from the ground. It was probably the biggest bluff in the history of mankind.

——

All of our ships are unarmed. There is no fighting going on in space — President Kennedy was right about that part — there is no armed conflict in space. Well, at least not here.

Our pilots were scared out of their wits — they were flying fast so that no one could catch them and shoot at them — they had no way to defend themselves! The best "attack" they could have possibly leveled on an Earth city would have been to drop buckets of water on one from low orbit. Believe me, they would *never* even do *that* — the cargo is far too precious!

Actual headline from the Washington Post

Anyway, as Adam has told me, the CIA became bored with his descriptions of these low orbital truck drivers—the same term by the way that Buzz Aldrin once used to describe your Space Shuttle Astronauts. If only Mr. Aldrin knew what was really going on up here!

We do admire Buzz Aldrin very much. How brave of him to set foot on Danaides III in that flimsy spacesuit he was wearing. It was so daring of him! Even our bravest technicians wouldn't do that on the surface that way.

We have always wondered though, why Earthlings call him "Buzz". Does he hear sounds in his head? Such a shame, such a brave man!

(Author's note: Aldrin picked up the name when his little sister mispronounced the word' brother' as 'buzzer.' The label stuck and was later shortened to Buzz. He later legally changed his name to 'Buzz'.)

Anyway eventually Project Blue Moon was decommissioned due to indifference. Adam was recalled and returned to translating Greek at the CIA.

Both the CIA and the Sirians felt safe with Adam holding their secret. Who would believe his story anyway? He is just another one of those conspiracy guys that can't prove a thing. The world was well for everyone. That is until the day I arrived at Adam's home with the news.

Why was I chosen to deliver the news? That is simple enough. No one else would go. Sirians are a pleasant people — we don't like bad news. No one wants to be the bearer of bad news on Sirius.

Scientists from Sirius have been stationed on Danaides III for years studying the Earth. In particular they have been interested in your global warming. This is an unusual phenomenon that is unique to Earth — no other inhabited planet that we know of is going through this peculiar event.

Even stranger are the phenomena that you know as aurora australis and aurora borealis — southern and northern lights that our Sirian scientists agree seem to be connected to the phenomena of global warming.

I arrived at Adam's doorstep with the news that the riddle of global warming was solved by our Sirius scientists. I suppose that was the good news. The bad news was the cause of the warming.

I hardly know how to put this because like I said Sirians hate bad news. But someone has to share the news. Adam tried to share the news too. Adam took this information to the CIA and unfortunately they laughed in his face. They thought that he was returning to his conspiracy roots so they didn't take him seriously. He begged and he begged but they wouldn't listen.

So Adam and I decided the best way to break the news was to come clean with the whole story from start to finish so that the whole world would understand. It would be easier that way for everyone involved. So that is why we came forward with this book. There, I hope you understand now.

Oh, the cause of the global warming? Well remember that Tetron energy facility at Coeus Major that I previously mentioned? Well it seems that we forgot to power it down before we left. You have to remember that our people were fleeing for their lives. We were in such a hurry — we had no time for such mundane things.

———

Anyway the reactor at Coeus Major had 10 times the amount of Tetron that was in the facility at the Eurybia Highlands and, well, you remember what happened there. Evidently they were expecting to do some intense mining at Coeus Major so they needed the extra power and so they put in an order for a super-sized shipment of Tetron when the plant was built. The facility has been running without supervision now for centuries and for the last 100 years the heat has been building up to a critical level.

Our scientists have determined that those heat emissions are what are causing the ice field to melt at Antarctica and the build-up of heat in your atmosphere. At some point the ice at Coeus Major will completely melt and it will expose the ground where the crater was dug to house the facility.

I suppose at that point the world will know the whole truth about the events that have occurred on Earth. Unfortunately that ice is what has kept the Tetron from critical heat levels for all of these years.

Oh, I almost forgot. What is the bad news? Well, after much consideration and research by the scientists who examined the problem from every angle we have determined that when the Tetron powered energy facility overheats there is going to be what might be called another "Extinction Event" right there on planet Earth.

As such we have advised the CIA that it is best to evacuate the planet as soon as possible so as to minimize the loss of life.

We are currently activating our evacuation plan on Danaides III so you need not worry about our personnel stationed there — they will be safely out of the blast zone by the time that it occurs.

Mission patch from ill-fated Apollo 13

CHAPTER 14
DANAIDES XIII

You are probably wondering why an advanced civilization such as the Sirians wouldn't just come down to Earth and take care of the technical oversight that has occurred at Coeus Major. To the mind of humans these things can seem so simple while in fact far more complex issues are at play.

History is filled with attempts of Sirians to interfere with the affairs of other races. As a result of our experiences our Committee on Off World Affairs must now carefully consider the potential consequences of any such endeavor before any action is taken.

This policy is a result of two historical events in Sirian history that have shaped our off world policy.

The first and most important event is the Tri-Universal Treaty. This treaty is an agreement between Sirius, Arke, and Cercopes not to interfere in off world matters — particularly when mining and water rights are involved. Historically these actions have generally proven to be unwise.

There is of course no actual written and signed treaty. It is more of a loosely held understanding between our races based upon a handshake that may have occurred in the distant past. We have always suspected that both Arke and Cercopes have violated the treaty on occasion and it is the reason we have tried to have all future treaties in writing.

Our new policy was evidenced by our strongly worded written agreement with President Nixon that was delivered by Michael Collins of your Apollo 11. It was so nice of the President to deliver the agreement to us in a vehicle named after our great leader Apollo — I must say that our bureaucrats were very greatly impressed by this kind gesture on your part.

We did find such a wonderful kindred spirit in Richard Nixon. A man that we supremely trusted who seemed to understand us as much as we understood him. Why can't all of your presidents be more like him?

The second event that also factored into our policy was the misfortunate incident at Danaides XIII. After the Ice Age commenced on Earth our scientists agreed that conditions were too hostile on Earth to continue operations — including the water extraction efforts. As a result the successful Danaides project was extended to a universal effort to find water supplies elsewhere.

The same process that created Danaides III was repeated on successive ventures. As our scientists often say, "Why mess with perfection?" Our ships continued to search the universe for gold and water resources as the Danaides project expanded.

It was the continuing Danaides project that led our highly advanced civilization to Cercopes. Prior to Cercopes the Danaides projects had all been successful finding gold and Tetron for extraction — but little or no water. When we found the Cercopes system we were more than delighted to finally find another source of the precious fluid of life.

The original Cercopes planetary system had a planet flowing with water unlike we had ever seen. The civilization of Cercopes was confined to two inner planets while Cercopes III was an outer planet — a pristine water world teaming with aquatic life.

The unfortunate events on Earth led us to feel an obligation to negotiate with Cercopes I and Cercopes II for water rights on Cercopes III. Since the planets were not spacefaring at that time we offered our Goldenite engine technology in exchange for exclusive water rights on Cercopes III.

We were quite proud of this masterful trade which at the time was considered one of the great accomplishments of Sirius. It was to assure us of plenty of water while at the same time we set the Cercopes people free to explore the heavens.

Cercopes I immediately incited a war with Cercopes II over some silly thing that we know nothing about. While the two planets argued over some arcane issue we constructed Danaides XIII so as to begin our water extraction on Cercopes III.

Danaides XIII was to be the grandest achievement ever conceived on Sirius. The titanic Danaides XIII was three times the size of Danaides III. Like the predecessors in the awe-inspiring Danaides series the massive orb was constructed from the rings of Sirius while in orbit.

Danaides XIII was fitted with twin Goldenite engines—both the largest ever constructed by Sirians up until that time. The finest siphoning equipment ever conceived was loaded into her landing bays and once again with the entire planet watching the massive sphere was piloted towards a grand entrance at Cercopes III.

What happened afterwards is seldom discussed on Sirius. The commander of Danaides XIII reported a minor navigational malfunction upon arriving in the Cercopes system. Tragically Danaides XIII met an untimely end with a high speed collision with Cercopes III while traveling well in excess of light speed. All hands on Danaides XIII—20,000 souls in all—were lost.

It was the first and only time to date that two Goldenite engines powered by Tetron had simultaneously exploded in flight.

Our technicians are very safety minded. When engaging in future projects engineers have made sure to never put two such large sized engines together again in one space vehicle for safety purposes.

Needless to say the impact of the vessel on Cercopes III was catastrophic to the newly discovered water world. Sadly the premier water resource in the universe was lost forever in the collision.

Almost equally disturbing was that the people of Cercopes misinterpreted the tragic loss of Danaides XIII. While we saw the event as a terrible regrettable accident they saw it as an act of war. As a result, very unfortunately, Cercopes vowed eternal vengeance on the people of Sirius for the loss of Cercopes III and this remains to this day the reason why we seldom speak of the incident.

CHAPTER 15
COVENANT OF ARKE

There are other historical events where advanced civilizations have reached out to inferior races and the results have not been optimal. Just to prove that these events are not unique to Sirius I can share events that occurred as a result of actions taken by the people of Arke on your very own planet.

As I have said the Arkians speak Latinus, are reasonably intelligent, have an odd sense of humor, and are highly spiritual. Should you come across Latinus anywhere in the universe you can be sure Arkians have been there — they have a habit of leaving behind things inscribed with the dreadful language.

Arkians discovered Tetron propulsion technology about the same time as Sirians, though they will tell you that we were still in cosmic diapers when they were out exploring the universe. They are of course incorrect. They are way too proud of the achievements of their race even though they are not all technological achievements — they have dabbled in many other areas as well.

It may or may not be true but yes, some say that the Arkians were first to be spacefaring. Their other achievements include discovery of eight of the ten elements not found on Earth, the invention of Pladonite—a somewhat important alloy and energy source, the location of the origin of life in the universe, and the scientific confirmation of the existence of God.

For some reason they are particularly proud of their irrefutable scientific evidence of the existence of God. We have never been impressed with their findings as the existence of God was self-evident and needed no further explanation to us.

Yet they flaunt this knowledge in the face of other races and are enamored with promoting religion through their influence. As a result you are most likely to find Arkians lurking in space ports handing out flowers and written tidbits of scripture in Latinus. Let's face it, nobody likes a self-righteous Arkian.

In the past they have often attempted to "enlighten" lessor races and it was sometimes met with unexpected results. Insidiously the Arkians would contact races and gain their confidence before attempting to push religion on them. Such was the case when the Arkians arrived on planet Earth and attempted to enlighten the planet.

The first thing that they did on Earth was promise great things with your indigenous population. After they struck an agreement to provide knowledge in exchange for people listening to their dreadfully boring lectures they then set up a communications link to remotely provide the lectures and advance and promote their ten rules for better living.

All of this arrangement was made in the Latinus language so it should be no surprise that misunderstandings occurred. The Arkians were attempting to make a deal—a "Covenant With Arke" as they say on Arke. It was supposed to be a trade of enlightenment from Arke in exchange for a captive audience and no more than that. Yes, their dreadful lectures are so boring that they need an agreement in order to have people consent to listen!

However your people didn't translate correctly and construed the agreement as "The Ark Of the Covenant"-- they even spelled "Arke" wrong-- thereby setting in motion a typical Arkian mess.

The transmitter was encased in gold—not Goldenite like our superior technology. Rather than using our superior Tetron as a power source they used their usual Pladite power source. Things went downhill from there as soon the humans discovered that the thing radiated energy when it was used.

From there the humans took initiative and mounted the transmitter on poles so that it was portable and immediately began using it as a weapon for use in warfare. In this case the joke was on the Arkians—their attempt to push their peaceful religion on the people of Earth resulted in a deadly weapon of war used with tragic consequences.

It is because of events like these that our Committee on Off World Affairs must approve our actions before we interfere in the affairs of other planets.

CHAPTER 16
CAVEAT ATTEMPTOR
(Let The Tryer Beware)

The dire situation on Earth at Coeus Major was in fact brought before our Committee on Off World Affairs. The Committee consists of 32 members and of course unanimous consent is required to take action. One would think that unanimous consent from a mere 32 member committee would be easily achieved but in fact this is not always the case on Sirius.

Sadly our scientists made a valiant effort to persuade the Committee to take action — and in a close vote it was decided not to interfere in matters on Earth. It was only after this consequence that a secret group on Danaides III decided to take matters into their own hands.

It was decided by the secret group that the best course of action would be to detonate the Tetron energy generator before it had a chance to achieve the critical heat level which would cause a much greater explosion. The group concluded that the logic behind creating an explosion to prevent an explosion appeared to be both brilliant and flawless.

A pre-emptive explosion at Coeus Major would give Earth a 75% probability of retaining its water and leaving the planet as a serviceable environment for continued liquid extraction. With only a 25% probability of what we would call an "unfortunate loss" the group decided to go ahead with the mission.

As the Tetron detonator was being loaded into one of our CV's Danaides III received a message that an Arke ship transporting an ambassador was approaching with an urgent message regarding the planet below. Operations were halted as we waited for the emissary from Arke to arrive.

The events that followed have since obtained mythical status. Various interpretations can be made depending upon which version of the story that you believe. Since action by Sirius was forbidden by the Committee on Off World Affairs I am prohibited from commenting further.

I, Cassandra Hera, will only say that due to the heroic actions taken by Sirians that the Earth was saved and water extraction thankfully continues. I will speak no more of the matter.

We are currently advised that an emissary from Arke has approached you to speak. They cannot be trusted and should not be believed. They are an arrogant race that thinks way too highly of themselves. As we always say of them, *Pompous Maximus*. I will speak no more of the matter.

(Authors note: *Pompous Maximus* is best left not translated).

The story continues with Adam Smith now commenting.

This is Adam Smith again. At this point we arrive at the end of the remarks that were made regarding the Danaides III conspiracy by Cassandra Hera. No doubt we will all sleep better at night knowing that the Sirians are keeping a close eye on our world.

The story should and would end there—except that as preparation for publication of Project Blue Moon was in process a mysterious emissary from Arke—named Claudia Quinta--arrived here to speak with me.

She spoke only in Latinus. The reader is cautioned that my ability to translate Latinus is not extraordinary—it is all Greek to me. However, I have made every effort to translate correctly so that the rest of the story can be told. She insisted that certain phrases be presented in their original Latinus. In those cases I have also provided translation. As you might expect these off-world sources are difficult to work with so I can only try to do my best.

I found her at my doorstep in a flowing white robe accompanied by two scribes who appeared intent on writing down every word she uttered. While I attempted to take photographic evidence of the event when I checked my digital camera after the fact I found that no pictures survived the encounter.

Apparently there is another side of this story that needs to be told—the events that occurred after the Arke ship arrived on Danaides III. Since the Sirians would not comment further we only have the story as told by the Arkians.

The remainder of the information presented here was relayed by Claudia Quinta of Arke. She not only approached me with the story--she was also on board the Arkian ship that arrived on the Moon at the previously mentioned fateful moment in time. As you will note she tells a slightly different version of the events.

The physical appearance of Claudia Quinta is hardly alien. Like Cassandra Hera she looks much like many women on Earth. She has flowing blonde hair and blue eyes. I suppose she could be mistaken for Helen of Troy with her beauty. She has a glow about her—she seems to radiate a goodness that makes you want to smile upon her first impression.

Here is her description of events as they occurred.

CHAPTER 17
UNIUS POTESTAS
(The Power Of One)

My name is Claudia Quinta of Arke. I bring
greetings from the great and noble planet of Arke
to all who wish to be enlightened with wisdom
from the knowledge of the Arkians. We
understand your need to know--as we know
there is need--and we provide when we can.

No doubt you wonder why I look so much like
your race. We are all from One Source so it
should be of no surprise to you. There is no
mystery there — we are all from One Source.

I was sent as an emissary to Danaides III and
have previously intervened on behalf of the
people of Arke into the events that were about to
take place on the planet Earth.

Those events would never come to the attention
of Earth if not for the publication of the book
Project Blue Moon which we have reviewed--prior
to publication--on Arke and found to be, shall we
say, a stretch of the truth.

Please listen carefully. I am only a messenger to planet Earth. I am only here to relay a message. I have no interest in attacking your planet. Please I beg you do not kill the messenger as your people are so apt to do. Listen and learn. Veritas Vos Liberabit. *(Translation: The Truth Will Set You Free.)*

Clearly the knowledge contained in *Project Blue Moon* is propaganda from Sirius which was intended to boast of alleged Sirian actions while omitting the deeds of the Arkian race. I am here to tell Earth the truth about the Sirians and I can assure you that the truth will set you free. Yes but Quid est veritas? *(What is Truth?)*

I will now attempt to enlighten you as to the true intentions of the Sirians. The deepest conspiracy of Danaides III is not the presence of the hollow sphere that is in orbit around your planet. A spacecraft is a spacecraft regardless of its size. The conspiracy is the *purpose* of Danaides III.

Let me tell you first of the Arkians. It is important that you know who is speaking before you listen to those who speak. We are often misrepresented by the Sirians because they have no faith in who we are and what we do.

Yes we have a sense of humor — what is life if there is no fun in it? But don't let our approach confuse you — we celebrate the good in the universe and the joy of life but we are also quite scientific in our ways.

Our artists are renown throughout the universe. Even on your planet we have left behind beautiful sculptures though your people do not recognize them as such.

The artists had so much fun on Rapa Nui; I believe you call it Easter Island, with the Moai figurines that they could hardly contain their creative urges. Surrounded by so much water how could they not be inspired?

Such beautiful artwork! Did you notice the figures gazing to the heavens? Such artistic expression! Simply magnificent!

The Moai on Easter Island

We think of ourselves as the inspiration for good in the universe — we like to watch how other races interact and then we act to counter evil and wrong doing as best as we can. We do not intercede with armies or force. As Earth has yet to learn, there are no winners or losers in war — only survivors. War is pointless and therefore we do not engage in it.

We do however believe in the Power of One — that one person can take action and that the consequence of events caused by one soul can ripple across the universe like a stone thrown into a pond. Think of an endless stream of dominos falling all caused by a simple touch.

Can you see how powerful one single action can be? One person can easily move mountains and achieve what armies cannot.

We can cite many examples of our actions even on your own Earth. We have shown how great the Power of One is. An emissary once left behind a simple blue print on the ground and your own people raised a great sculpture of their own!

The pyramids of Egypt

We have also sent emissaries from time to time to tip events in the direction of good. While some of them are long since gone others continue to impact your world even today.

Here are just a few of them—judge our intentions by their actions and know the truth for yourself what the Power of One can be and what the intentions of Arke are on your planet:

Mahatma Gandhi—Sent to bring peace to the Earth.
Albert Einstein—Sent to advance the Earth.
Edgar Cayce—Sent to enlighten the Earth.
Jonas Salk—Sent to heal the Earth.

These are just a few. There were many others—I could go on and on. You would be surprised.

We have watched your planet both up close and at a distance for quite some time. On occasion we might choose not to send an emissary but instead we simply whisper into the ear of the right person at the right time. Oh the Power of One!

Yes we whispered into the ear of George Washington and a nation was born. We are the greenies of whom he wrote. He misinterpreted the glow of our ships as the color of our skin. My ancestors did us proud at Valley Forge!

(Authors note: At a critical moment in history George Washington wrote in his diary of glowing green beings he called the "greenies" that showed him the vision of America that he was going to help create. Inspired he confidently continued the war that others thought a lost cause--and a new nation was born.)

On other occasions we spoke to authors. For instance we tried to explain things to Erich Von Daniken. We thought a message conveyed by one of the purveyors of such fine time pieces would certainly be believed worldwide. But it wasn't so. So much for the precision of a Swiss watch. The world scoffed at the truth!

(Authors note: Swiss author Erich Von Daniken wrote the book Chariots of the Gods in which he promoted the ancient astronaut theory.)

We realize that there are difficulties speaking with your people as you do not speak the heavenly language of the cosmos which of course is Latinus. Our history with your world includes many miscommunications as a result of your poor ability to translate. Your children should stop playing video games and stay in school. Have them learn something useful like Latinus!

In one of our early ventures we tried to urge the people of Earth to take action against the Sirians. Our emissary implored them to Carpe Diem! *(Seize the day!)* In an episode that would foreshadow difficult relations with our world our emissary was immediately fed a fish dinner. This occurred over and over as we attempted to instill a sense of urgency in the people of your planet.

It was many Earth years before we realized that our cry was translated incorrectly. We did not realize that carp was a fish that swam in your bodies of water. While our warning was unheeded at least we enjoyed the day.

Quite a tasty fish I might add as I have personally enjoyed the delicacy on many occasions on your planet. Yes, we have all been misunderstood many times.

CHAPTER 18
VENI VIDI VICI
(I Came I Saw I Conquered)

Your history is filled with the actions of evil. Incidentally you should know that many of these actions were not all of your own making.   There are some in the universe that misuse the Power of One to achieve their own objectives.

In particular I am referring to the Cercopes people and their intentions in the grand scheme of things. They are all unclean souls with evil intent. Better that Cercopes should bring an army and stage an invasion than for you to deal with their Power of One trickery. They routinely misuse their power. At least if any army were to arrive your planet would know who and what it is fighting.

To spy a Cercopes ship in orbit around your planet is akin to having a buzzard circling above waiting to feast on wounded prey. The bird is a scavenger — it only waits to take advantage of the situation that develops beneath it. This is the Cercopes people. They build nothing and they leave nothing.

You can be sure that those from Cercopes always have the same intent—to cause war, destruction, and confusion and in the chaos claim everything for themselves and their empire. No trick is beneath them or any loss of life too much for them to tolerate. Sometimes they make grand gestures while other times they are subtle while attempting to benefit in the long run.

You have been visited many times by agents from Cercopes. Fortunately your planet survived each massacre as we were there every time to be sure that the interlopers failed.

Genghis Kahn, Napoleon Bonaparte, and Adolf Hitler are terrible but obvious examples of sordid efforts that Cercopes agents made to cause direct conflict in war. An interesting strategy don't you think? Incite the war and sit back and watch the carnage.

Such abuse of the Power of One! Do you know your own history? In Adolph Hitler your world discovered for itself what misuse of this power can bring. While their ships observed in orbit millions were destroyed on your planet in a mindless quest for control of your planet.

In the end only one soul from Cercopes was lost in the battle—even then he took his own life for his failure to accomplish his mission. Just one agent from Cercopes—Hitler—almost destroyed your entire world!

They also made other attempts—much more subtle I should say--to change the course of human history. We didn't know what to make of Karl Marx—a devious mind from Cercopes--intent on changing your governments around the globe.

Communism is the opposite of the Power of One. Capitalism celebrates the individual and the achievement of freedom. What an insidious attempt to undermine your world this was!

Communism sinks to the level of a committee—always the least efficient way to advance civilization. Communism, like a committee, always proceeds at the pace of the slowest member—thus always assuring inefficiency. This is the only true way to defeat the Power of One—to have a group think for you and decide your fate for you.

What were we to do with Communism and the Cercopes agent Karl Marx? In that particular instance we threw our hands up in frustration. The Power of One cannot be easily defeated but it can be made impure. Finally we decided not to take this folly seriously — we were sure it would collapse upon its own weight.

I guess we never took Karl as a legitimate threat. In jest we eventually countered the movement of Karl Marx by dispatching the Marx Brothers. Surely you didn't think that Groucho was of your world? We do have a sense of humor on Arke which I hope you can appreciate.

Please — there is no need — to credit us with the Three Stooges. I can assure you that they were yours though we were quite envious on Arke.

Cercopes has also made every attempt possible to thwart the Earth landings on Danaides III. They realized the significance of your people learning about the Sirians and so they wanted to keep the event from ever happening.

You should know that Lee Harvey Oswald was an agent from Cercopes. He was accompanied by five other Cercopes agents in Dealey Plaza so the fate of your President was sealed. Their mission was to attempt to foil your entire space effort by eliminating your President.

The theory on Cercopes was that the new administration would stop the project once the biggest supporter of the effort was eliminated. A miscalculation I should say on the part of the interlopers.

The Cercopes fools underestimated the resolve of your planet. Their action only made the Danaides III landings that much more inevitable. Good will always thwart evil — it is the way of things. The people of Cercopes have never learned.

Cercopes intervention did not stop there. Any review of the Russian space program that was also directed at reaching Danaides III has to result in suspicion. All of those faulty launches were not accidental. Cercopes had decided in advance that conditions would be better for them if the Americans reached Danaides III first so they made sure that was the case.

CHAPTER 19
CAVE FATUOS
(Beware Of The Fools)

You should know and respect that the Arkians are the guardians of the universe. Our values and actions are thought of quite highly throughout the known universe. We are probably thought of the same in the unknown universe as well — we do think so — but that is unknown. If it were known then we would know that.

You should know who you are in league with when you deal with the Sirians. You should know that your quid pro quo (*this for that*) signed by your President and delivered by Apollo 11 made you the laughing stock of the universe.

While we monitored your actions and as your astronaut was proclaiming "One small step for a man, one giant leap for mankind" the cosmos were hysterically laughing. I mean really, we thought it should be more like "One small step for a man, one giant mistake for mankind."

Did the Sirians mention that nobody had ever signed an agreement with them before — that you were the first and only? We couldn't believe what we were seeing!

There is a reason for this. Nobody signs anything with the Sirians. They cannot be trusted. They are the pirates of the universe — they pillage, plunder, and steal without thought of the consequence. Most planets do not survive the carnage of a deal with the Sirians written or otherwise. It was difficult for us to imagine that the Earth would be the first to do so.

Perhaps of all the races in the universe the Sirians are considered the most dangerous — they are devious and certainly not what they appear to be. The Sirians are known throughout the universe as pirates and thieves. You should know who you are dealing with before you deal. They are also the most pompous self-absorbed fools in the universe.

Their Goldenite engines are a technological disgrace. After the incident with Danaides XIII we tried to get them to buy our Pladite engines but they were far too proud to do that. At one point we even tried to give them our Pladite engines if only for the sake of the safety of the universe but they still declined.

Your world traded away the most valuable commodity in the universe for a few mere technological baubles. You received computers, cell phones, flat panel television, basic genetics, and microwave ovens when you could have had the secret of gravity, faster than light space travel, and an unlimited source of clean power from something the size of a small grain of sand!

Then look at the dangers of what you have received. Sirians have done you no favor with your "windfall" of technology.

Beware the emissions from your cell phones. Beware the radiation that contaminates your food from your microwave ovens.

Most of all beware the most the effects of genetic manipulation. This is a genie that the Sirians have let out of the capsule on your planet. Think of the previous users of genetic manipulation on your planet — the Nazis — and what it brought them to.

Are you aware that your planet has already been the subject of a massive genetic experiment by the Sirians? Of course not — but upon further investigation res ipsa loquitur! *(The Matter speaks for itself.)*

Haven't you ever wondered how odd the variations of your people are? Some are tall, some are short, dark hair, fair hair. All sorts of color of eyes. Such variety is not found elsewhere in the universe.

They tinkered with your animals too. Your camel was their first attempt at an improved horse — as designed by the Sirian Off World Committee!

Genetic manipulation is banned throughout the universe but practiced only by the Sirians, the Cercopes Nazi minions, and your scientists today. The secret of their past manipulations can be found in the teeth. Those with wisdom teeth and those without tell the story. Nota bene! *(Note well!)*

Do you realize what will become of your world? Those who do not learn the lessons of history are doomed to repeat it. Without enlightenment your civilization is doomed! Simply look to the sky to see for yourselves what awaits your world with help from your friends from Sirius.

No, look not to the Moon, but to your father planet — look to Mars to see the truth of the Sirians. It is why we tried to lure your NASA there with the facial sculpture that we left behind. Clever don't you think?

History records that Mars was such a picturesque planet! Our ships once stopped there just to view the vast oceans and breathe the sweet air! The exquisite canals of Mars were the envy of the galaxy. Mars was once a thriving planet with beautiful people and cities.

I have read of the perfect seasons that Mars had. Those long summers and short winters in the North were the coveted by all. I understand that the water never froze and tourists would arrive year round.

Our history tells of a most wonderful people who were meant to live among the stars. Elaborate buildings and observatories like the universe had never seen. It has all been covered with dust.

All that remains is the tip of the great temple. It peers from the dust like the ghost of a long lost civilization.

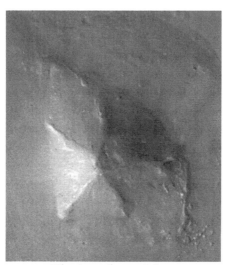

The temple on Mars

They were far too generous—much too naive.
The people of Mars never realized what
happened to them. After the Sirians caused your
ice age the Sirians arrived on Mars and
plundered their water supply—it was sold for
quite a price on the black market and the Sirians
profited well from it.

Foolish Earthlings! The Sirian gold mining was just a diversion — a bonus for their efforts. The true prize is your water — they will take it all and leave you with nothing. Why settle for a quarter of the water when you can simply take it all! They have a scorched planet policy — take it all and leave nothing behind! How will you stop it? You will never know or realize what has happened until it is over.

How can you know that I am telling the truth? Look to the sky, see Mars for yourself. We have even marked the way for you.

NASA has seen the monolith that we left on Phobos to point you in the right direction. Even your Apollo astronaut Buzz Aldrin has said the monolith is significant — he knows the truth!

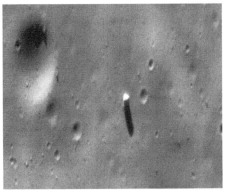

Monolith on Phobos

The monoliths are historical markers. They have been placed so that future generations may learn from history. Those who fail to learn from history are doomed to repeat it. Approach the marker and you will learn the story that lies behind its placement.

What are Earthlings waiting for — an illuminated billboard? The only time your people go anywhere is when they are forbidden to do so! We thought that the monolith would be enough to draw even the least curious of spacefarers — even the people of Earth.

Just to be sure you didn't miss the invitation we left a monolith on Mars too.

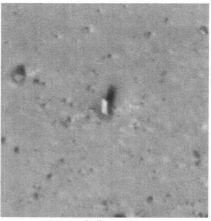

Monolith on Mars

You know that it is there — your NASA has photographed Phobos. Now go see Mars and Phobos for yourselves. Have NASA go there and learn the truth. It is fittingly so for I will now reveal the greatest secret of all.

Where did the Martians go when their world was destroyed? What remained of the beautiful people who lived on Mars?

As their atmosphere was thinned by the Sirians and dissipated into space what few who were able took what they could and scrambled to their spacecraft.

We did all that we would to help. We took hundreds ourselves as quickly as we could to the beautiful sister planet. It pained us to watch a world end but we could not save it.

As the Sirians watched a civilization of millions was thinned to hundreds. Only a few could escape in the limited number of ships that they had that were capable of space flight. We did the best that we could to help.

Those fortunate enough to survive came here — to Earth and to the sister planet. People of Earth, You are the Martians; you are the descendants of those who had their beautiful world destroyed by the Sirians!

Have you not noticed that the human sleep cycle is not set to the 24 hours of the Earth day? Does this not make you suspicious? Haven't you been curious as to why this is so?

It is set to the Martian day! You need no further fact to prove the truth. The Martian day is 40 minutes longer than on Earth. Your average sleep cycle of humans is set to a longer period than your 24 hours — it is off on Earth by about 40 minutes — what does that tell you? Your own biorhythms scream to the heavens and betray your origin!

You should know what your civilization represents to the rest of us. The people of Earth stand today as the prime example to the universe ad nauseam *(to the point of disgust)* of what the Sirians do to other worlds.

The irony should not be lost. A once great spacefaring people now needs an invitation to return to the stars. How sad the course of events has been!

Forewarned is forearmed! Danaides III does ring like a bell when it is struck. Ask not for whom the bell tolls, it tolls for thee!

Ask the Sirians about Danaides VI thru Danaides XII. I haven't even mentioned Danaides XXV. You have no need to ask of Danaides IV and V — they are both in plain view left abandoned in orbit around Mars — a testament to the plundering greed of the Sirians.

Your people call them Phobos and Deimos. Yes somebody knew the truth on Earth at one time! Phobos represents panic and fear. Deimos terror and dread. Look it up and see for yourself!

Yes the Sirians were so greedy — in such a hurry-- to pillage beautiful Mars that they sent contingents in two ships to complete the task before anyone else could stop them. They were made smaller for deception. Even today they are too small for NASA to bother with — mission accomplished--conspiracy complete!

CHAPTER 20
THE SISTER PLANET

We are so sorry for the fate of those on the sister planet. Our race feels our guilt to this day. We helped to transport all of those Martians there. It was such a beautiful world. Your second planet was the envy of the universe.

We transported all of those people—hundreds of them—to the blue planet with the inviting lush green fields. It is hard to believe now but Venus was an upgrade over both the Earth and the Martian environments. Venus was the shining world of your system.

Our history records the events. As our ships left them behind we felt so happy for the survivors of Mars. We could not save them all but we did our part the best that we could.

They thrived on the lush planet building elaborate cities powered by our Platonite energy generators. They were spacefaring as well and they sold their goods across the galaxy.

We didn't know. We just didn't know. Oh, sins of the fathers! May God forgive us and all of our descendants. We didn't know.

Author's note: At this point Claudia began to sob and weep. It was a few moments before she composed herself and could continue.

The story has been told through the generations on Arke and it still saddens us each time that it is retold. I am so sorry, we do not bear this burden well.

Such a beautiful moon Venus had. Yes, Venus had a moon back then. It was much bigger than your Moon and it glowed a heavenly sight in the night sky. How were we to know that such a beautiful orb was part of the Danaides project?

When the Tetron generator on Danaides XXV malfunctioned the end was at least quick for the unfortunate inhabitants of Venus. In moments Danaides XXV disintegrated, permanently changing the orbit of Venus and vaporizing its atmosphere.

In an instant all life was gone on Venus. A civilization consumed in a flash. All that was good was gone. Intense heat obliterated any evidence that life once proudly walked on the beautiful world.

How were we to know that the Danaides treachery was so widespread? We had no knowledge then of the Moon around Venus. We were fooled just like you have been.

Now Venus has no moon and it has no life. It can never be what it was. Now it floats through the sky a shell of the beauty that it used to be. Even the Power of One couldn't save your doomed sister planet.

CHAPTER 21
ALLY
SOCIUS

You should know that this information has been previously shared before with your people on Earth but has been kept secret from the multitudes. Those enlightened among you wish to keep the population from panicking in the face of possible extinction. We are not without partners in our work as guardians.

Perhaps you have heard of the Vatican and the works that go on there. They are the guardians of this knowledge on Earth and details are kept in their secret Vatican library.

You should ask why no one is allowed inside the secret library. Is knowledge so dangerous that it needs to be guarded? This should be suspicious all by itself. Of course they have all been sworn to protect this information and have dutifully kept the secrets through the ages.

They are good people there and we trust them. Most on are unaware of the sacred duty they have been sworn to in order to protect planet Earth. At our request the Vatican works to keep tabs on Sirian activity in this region of space. Sirians and Cercopians are so insidious that we can't seem to keep track of them on our own.

For this reason the Vatican owns and operates an advanced telescope often referred to as the "Popescope". We hope that you enjoy the levity of that moniker because it was our idea and we are quite proud of that! Hidden on Mount Graham in southwest Arizona the Vatican Observatory is one of the oldest astronomical observatories on your world attesting to the fact that we have been in contact with the Vatican for some time.

Popescope

Note the obscure location of this observatory. This facilitates the undetected landing of our ships when we choose to drop in and check with the findings. When we fly over your cities everybody seems to get all excited about it but when we land in your fields nobody seems to care.

It was the Vatican who notified us of the secret alliance between the Cercopians and the Nazis and it was only on account of this notification that we were able to intercede.

While the relationship between Hitler and astronomy is well known you may not know that we helped to end the fighting—we helped to end the war.

We sent Albert Einstein to warn of the danger and then we gave J. Robert Oppenheimer the secret of the atomic bomb when things got too far out of hand.

We regretted so much having to do so. There are no winners or losers in war—only survivors—as we have said. Oppenheimer himself learned too. "Now I am become Death, the destroyer of worlds". Good must always triumph over evil—no matter the price—it is the way of the universe.

Atomic Bomb

We have learned too. The Power of One is greater than the power of all. One is Nec pluribus impar (*not unequal to many*). You will learn that too.

Having enlightened with that powerful information I think I should have full disclosure in the interest of complete honesty and integrity. A relationship between worlds must be based on truth.

Your world is so wonderful that it boasts of some of the finest fruits and vegetable in the known universe. Our scientists have proclaimed it is because of the abundance of water --which you now know is scarce away from your world.

Anyway it is a temptation that our pilots cannot seem to resist. Occasionally they will drop down onto a field of the scrumptious treats and help themselves to a few tasty morsels. It would seem to be small payment for our services as guardians of your world and of the galaxy.

Anyway, in true Arkian tradition our pilots cannot just leave it at that. In sort of a form of cosmic graffiti they have often seen fit to leave behind reminders that they have visited. Once they realized what havoc this played with locals they simply couldn't resist.

So if you see any of their insignia in your fields— I believe you call them crop circles-- know that they are simply a gesture from your cosmic friends saying "Hello, we were here!" The insignia shown below was particularly humorous for our pilots as we certainly don't look like the caricature shown but we like to pretend to Earth that we do. Your people buy it every time!

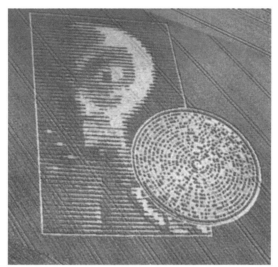

Alien Crop Circle

Some of your people have engaged in this same artistic form. We are flattered by the imitation of our artists. We have enlightened your people! The highest form of the Power of One!

CHAPTER 22
JE VOIS TOUT
(I See All)

Pardonnez-moi l'expression (*pardon my French*) —
we speak many languages in the words of the
species that we encounter and sometimes we mix
them up. It can be difficult for us to keep it all
straight. One of our emissaries once thought he
said "Let's keep our heads!" but somehow it
came out as "Off with her head!" These things
can happen in delicate cosmic matters and it is a
sad affair indeed when it does occur.

We find the French such a wonderful people.
What is not to like of wine, women, and song?
Apparently the French are so very fond of us as
they even carry our universal flag of purity into
battle.

Yes there is something so pure and most
wonderful to see a race carry the white flag of
Arke into battle with the purest of heart. Fighting
has often ceased and armies have been known to
lay down their arms at the sight of the
awesomeness of the flag of purity. Viva La
France!

As wonderful as French is so like so many languages it can be ambiguous. This is the reason that we speak in Latinus or Latin as your people call it. Latinus is extremely precise so no misinterpretation occurs. Well not very often anyway. There was the time we said "Latin is well read" and somebody translated it as "Latin is dead" but these things happen and we can forgive.

Besides, we have found without doubt that Quidquid latine dictum sit, altum sonatur. Or for those of you who have not been properly educated in the language of the cosmos this means "*Anything said in Latin sounds profound*". Wouldn't you agree?

Having given this background information I can proceed to the elements of the meeting on Danaides III that decided the fate of your planet. You should know that since the invention of our micro viewers that nothing transpires on Danaides III or in your White House without our knowledge.

The micro viewer is an ingenious invention of ours and we have many that allow us to keep tabs on everything that goes on regarding your world. The viewers are the size of the tip of a pin and can be hidden anywhere. We have over 1,000 of these in the conference room of the Sirian Off World Committee alone as well as over 10,000 of them in hidden in your White House.

The images--complete with full audio--are broadcast in real time to our entire fleet of ships as well as to our monitors on Arke so that no detail of interplanetary importance is missed.

While we are thinking of it please tell your President that he should have that left mandibular second molar looked at as it requires attention. Oh and also the First Lady need not worry about the tiny growth on her left…ah, let's just say it is a beauty mark that is not malignant and leave it at that.

I might also add that our monitors think that the First Lady is quite beautiful with or without her beauty mark. Yes she is a superb vision of Earthly womanhood. Our monitors never seem to be able to get enough of her.

While I think of it I must say that if you ever should visit the White House and desire privacy of your intimate features you may not want to visit any of the restrooms. Or the bedrooms for that matter.

Anyway back on Sirius the fate of your planet was being decided. Did the Sirians tell you the result of their debate regarding your dire state of affairs? The 32 member committee discussed your situation before voting on a proposal to stop water extraction and deal with the issue at Coeus Major.

As you know the purpose of all committees is to obfuscate, confuse, and delay action. In this sense the Sirian Off World Committee works very efficiently. Never forget that if you want something done always turn to the Power of One. The Sirians would seem to have proven this true.

The final vote included 17 abstentions as some members didn't feel that the meeting was important enough to attend. The present members voted 10 to 5 to extract all of the water as soon as possible and let the Tetron energy generator do whatever it will do. Or to put it in different terms, the vote was 27 to 5 let your world disintegrate.

———

We would have interfered at that moment but we knew of the efforts on Danaides III to save your world. We thought that perhaps someone from Sirius would finally take responsibility and act for the greater good. As you know we are optimists on Arke and we always presume that good will come from bad intentions.

In this particular case our faith was not rewarded. I suppose that even on Arke we can't win them all. The plan hatched on Danaides III was to destroy the Tetron energy generator but in the process render half of your planet uninhabitable. Since the water resource would still be available the Sirians on Danaides III considered this acceptable "collateral damage" and they were prepared to proceed.

As we like to say on Arke "A snake deserves no pity" so we immediately made the decision to intercede. You may thank us as you please.

It is unusual for an emissary from Arke to make a formal presentation to Sirians on Danaides III. Such work is normally done at a snail's pace through proper diplomatic channels on Arke or on Sirius.

However in this instance we felt that the situation demanded special consideration so as I said an emissary was sent.   A ship was deployed at top speed to Danaides III to explain the particulars of the situation on Earth.

Due to the unusual circumstances of this event we made sure that the meeting was simultaneously beamed back to Sirius as well as to over 200 other known planets. We wanted to make sure that the universe knew what Sirians had planned for your world.

Our quartz crystal antennae transmission technology assured us that the meeting would not remain private. We have placed the monolithic antennae everywhere — even on your own planet.

Our powerful transmitters can reach the entire known universe. In fact they are so powerful that even parts of the unknown universe probably witnessed the magnificent events on Danaides III as they unfolded. This way all could praise the Power of One and witness the glory of Arke!

CHAPTER 23
SUMMUM BONUM
The Highest Good

The conference room was quiet as our emissary prepared to speak. Then all of the events on Earth leading up to the forgotten Tetron energy generator were recounted for all of the civilizations to hear and record. An audible gasp could be heard throughout the known galaxy as we explained the condition of the Tetron energy generator and how the Sirians had recklessly abandoned the unit when they selfishly fled for their lives.

All races realized the implication of these actions — Earth was doomed and nothing could be done to save it. The Sirians were exposed for what they really were. The attempt to save Earth from Danaides III with a smaller Tetron detonation was in reality an attempt to cover up the truth. It was an attempt to once again hide the true dealings of those criminals from Sirius.

Conspiracy was revealed, the truth told, inter-galactic shame was brought upon the Sirians! Other races launched probes to their own Moons even as the meeting continued to make sure that they were indeed legitimate heavenly bodies and not a base of operations for the Sirians.

But the very best was yet to come. The Sirians —
they are so proud of themselves — so haughty!
They deserved what they got! They think that
they are the finest race in the universe and that
we must all fall beneath their conquest.

Their pathetic motto is "In hoc signo vinces"
which translates to *"In this sign thou wilt
conquer"* — the slogan is so proudly displayed on
the side of their space vehicles.

As the Sirians cowered in shame the universe
mourned for the inevitable loss of your planet.
Tears were shed for the loss of another beautiful
blue planet with all of its liquid resources.

It was then that we delivered the Coup de
grace — my French again — or the *mortal blow* to
the Sirians. For there is no greater shame — no
greater defeat — possible in the universe than to
become belittled as a result of being the butt of a
joke played on oneself. It is difficult if not
impossible to ever be taken seriously again as a
result.

To our delight there was universal laughter — snickering of the very most demeaning sort — as our emissary from Arke spoke and revealed the truth about the circumstance at Coeus Major. For there would be no explosion on Earth nor would there be an extinction of the Martian (Earth) race.

We explained that our observers had seen the events on Earth so many years ago that spawned your Ice Age. While the Sirians had fled your planet in fear our brave technicians flew their craft — at great danger — to Coeus Major. Working skillfully in the cold they had properly deactivated the Tetron generator thus rendering the unit harmless.

Of course being Arkians we could not leave it at that. We could not leave the Earth to become a cold and desolate world destined to become totally barren and encased in a frosty tomb. We could not leave the planet to that!

So we left behind at Coeus Major a small Platonite device which was designed to emit a warm glow as well as a beautiful magnetic energy field.

The warm glow was designed to gently warm your planet and return it to the natural state. The oceans of your planet rise because that is their natural level. The Polar Regions were ice free before the Sirians arrived—and they shall be again.

The magnetic energy field was our elegant signature—that we were there! The Power of One prevailed! A beacon to all of the universe of the glorious power of good in triumph over deceit and evil.

A continuous display of superb radiance the magnetic energy field is polarized to the ends of your planet. I believe you have seen the effect on Earth and you refer to it as aurora borealis in the north and aura australis in the south—also called northern lights and southern lights.

Quite a triumphant display of the glory of good we would most humbly say! Just like Danaides III the truth of Coeus Major was in plain sight—in view for all to see. Only the fools of Sirius couldn't see the truth through their greed and scientific ineptitude.

As we have spread our good across the universe we have marked our planets with similar beacons — to ward off the Sirians and to remind the universe of their folly.

We have acted summum bonum — *for the highest good*. We believe annuit coeptis-- *He has smiled on our undertakings*.

Northern Lights

CHAPTER 24
NOVOS ORDO SECLORUM
New Order Of The Ages

The phrase *Novos ordo seclorum* appears on the reverse of the Great Seal of the United States which was first designed in 1782. It has been printed on the back of the United States one-dollar bill since 1935.

Some conspiracy theorists think that this reads *A New World Order* which of course is an incorrect translation from Latinus. We don't really understand why that continues to happen but it is what it is. The correct translation is *New Order Of The Ages*.

The phrase was given to America by Benjamin Franklin--an emissary from Arke--in 1782. It was accepted by your Founding Fathers as a token to be displayed as gratitude for our assistance in forming a new nation of a most noble cause.

The buzz regarding "A new world order" is typical of how Arkians are misunderstood. We are a noble race with good intentions. We have no desire to invade your world — we are simply guardians of all that is good.

We also like to protect the precious water supplies of the universe. We do of course occasionally skim a bit of the liquid off of the top but who could blame us? So tempting and such a small price to pay for our enlightenment!

Also widely seen in the United States is "E pluribus enum" which translates correctly as "Out of one, many". Such a wonderful expression from your world! Sadly we did not think of this first—we had nothing to do with the creation of this wonderful phrase. Our scholars were impressed indeed by this brilliant proclamation.

The phrase was your idea—a welcoming gesture to us acknowledging our most noble creed "The Power of One". Well said! Bravo Earthlings!

Of course the New Order Of The Ages refers to wisdom overcoming deceit. The New Order Of The Ages refers to the efforts to overcome the deceit of the Sirians and the Cercopians and replace it with the greater good.

The New Order will be achieved through enlightenment. Knowledge is power! Advising planets of the intent of pirates like those from Sirius will serve to undermine their intentions and make the universe a much safer place from which to spread the word of all things good.

As you see our good words and deeds resonate through the ages. That which was good is still good and it echoes loudly today long after the sound of muskets and cannon fire has faded. The Power of One is formidable indeed!

I hope that you see *both sides now*. I hope that you look at the clouds differently as a result of the truth that was told here.

Tsiolkovskiy Crater

CHAPTER 25
EX POST FACTO
After the Deed

Adam Smith continues the story from here.

As Claudia finished those final words struck a chord with me. "Claudia, did you say *Both Sides Now*? Are you a Judy Collins fan too?"

"Oh yes," she replied. "Isn't everybody?"

"Celine Dione too. Such beautiful heavenly voices. As though listening to angels that came from heaven above. Do you enjoy their goodness — do you see it too — it radiates from them!"

"Claudia, did Arke send them here?"

"I can't reveal all of our secrets to you Adam. I can say however that we did send Jimmy Buffett to your world to enlighten and inspire. Something went dreadfully wrong with him though. We have never quite figured it out.

Our people believe that it had something to do with a place called Margaritaville. We would like to find out what happened there but our ships have been unable to locate the city. We are also interested in the cloaking technology that hides it from our view."

She smiled and gave me a playful wink and with that our interview ended.

She started humming a tune as she stepped off the porch and began walking away. I recognized it and the words came into my head as I smiled and listened. Who would ever think that aliens would listen to Judy Collins?

Bows and flows of angel hair
And ice cream castles in the air
And feather canyons everywhere
I've looked at clouds that way.

But now they only block the sun
They rain and snow on everyone
So many things I would have done
But clouds got in my way.

I've looked at clouds from both sides now
From up and down and still somehow
It's cloud's illusions I recall
I really don't know clouds at all.

Claudia then disappeared into the misty night with her two scribes in tow — they were still taking notes as she faded out of sight.

Shortly after Claudia Quinta left there was a knock at my front door. To my surprise there stood Cassandra Hera — a welcome friend whom I have long since come to trust.

I'm always amazed at how these people come and go. They always seem to know what is going on and they seem appear at just the right moment. When they enter it always makes me want to look out the window and check to see if there is a spacecraft parked out front. The times I checked there never was.

Cassandra told me that she had heard that the Arkians had tried to intervene in our world and that *Project Blue Moon* was going to be printed for all of Earth to read. She wanted to be sure that the Sirians had the opportunity to refute the lies that were being propagated by the people of Arke.

I warmly welcomed her into my home and she sat comfortably on the same couch where Claudia had just been seated. We began to discuss again the sequence of events that had taken place both on Danaides III and here on Earth.

She looked straight at me — I always could tell the truth of her words by her steady gaze when she talked. She was such a lovely woman and I knew that I could always count on her to be sincere and honest with me. How could I not trust her?

"I have so much more to tell you Adam — I will set the record straight for you today. There is no need to distribute the lies of Arke. Don't believe for a moment their story about the planet Venus. Their story about Mars isn't true either. They spread their version of the history of the cosmos as though they own the skies. Do not trust them for a moment.

I will admit that I may have stretched the truth with you just a bit and perhaps omitted a few minor facts. I'd like to have the chance to tell you the rest of the story."

She smiled as I gazed into those beautiful blue eyes. Who could resist such a tempting vision?

"But I've come such a long way to be here with you this evening. Before we start Adam, may I have a glass of water?"

Inscription left behind by Apollo 11

When researching Project Blue Moon it didn't take long to appreciate the relationship between the planet Sirius and many traditional Earth myths and legends. The odd striking coincidences lead to the inevitable conclusion that many things thought to be myth on Earth were in fact a result of true cosmic events.

The reader is helped here with by matching references made in Project Blue Moon with actual Earth legends.

AETHER
The Greek god of the upper air and light.

ARES
The Greek god of war, bloodshed, and violence. Moody and unreliable he generally represents the chaos of war.

ARKE
Messenger of the Titans.

CASSANDRA

In Greek mythology the red haired, blue eyed, fair skinned Cassandra was the daughter of King Priam and Queen Hecuba of Troy.

She was considered the second most beautiful woman in the world to Helen of Troy. Her beauty caused Apollo to grant her the gift of prophecy. When Cassandra refused Apollo's attempts at seduction he placed a curse on her so that her predictions and those of all of her descendants would not be believed.

Cassandra foresaw the destruction of Troy and warned the Trojans of the horse but was unable to do anything because no one believed her.

CERCOPES
In Greek mythology these were mysterious forest creatures who roamed the world and might turn up anywhere that mischief was afoot.

COEUS
Titan of intellect and the axis of heaven around which the constellations revolved.

DANAIDES
In Greek mythology there were 50 daughters of Danaus. They were to marry the fifty sons of Danaus's twin brother Aegyptus, a mythical king of Egypt.

All but one of the women killed their husbands on their wedding night and were condemned to spend eternity carrying water in a sieve or other perforated device. They come to represent the futility of a repetitive task that can never be completed.

DIONE
The oracle of Dodona.

DOLON
Fast runner who fought for Troy in the Trojan War.

EURYBIA
Titan of the mastery of the seas.

HERA
One of the three sisters of Zeus known for her jealous and vengeful nature.

NOMMO

Ancestral spirits worshipped by the Dogon tribe of Mali (see appendix B). The Nommos are usually described as amphibious fish-like creatures. Art depictions of the Nommos show creatures with humanoid upper torsos, legs/feet, and a fish-like lower torso and tail. They are also referred to as "Masters of the Water", "The Monitors", and "The Teachers".

OCEANUS
Titan of the all-encircling river oceans around the Earth, the font of all the Earth's fresh-water.

PERSES
Titan of destruction and of peace.

TETHYS
Titan mother of rivers, streams, fountains and clouds.

APPENDIX B
CORROBOLATING FACTS OF THE MATTER

In addition to mythological references Project Blue Moon includes many well-known historical facts. These facts are "main stream" — common knowledge not in dispute-- and can easily be verified in history books or even with a simple Google search.

Some of these are provided here for the benefit of the reader.

2002 AA29
A small near-Earth asteroid that revolves around the sun in an orbit very similar to that of Earth.

3753 Cruithne
Is an asteroid in orbit around the sun that relative to Earth is in a bean-shaped orbit. It occasionally is referred to as "Earth's second Moon."

APOLLO 11
Landed on the Moon on July 20, 1969 and man first walked on the Moon on July 21, 1969. Command module pilot Michael Collins remained in orbit during the Moon landing.

CHICXULUB CRATER

A prehistoric impact crater buried deep beneath the Yucatan Peninsula in Mexico. Believed to possibly be the cause of the dinosaur extinction.

HARRY S. TRUMAN
The White House was in fact buzzed by UFO's on July 19, 20, 26, and 27 of 1952 when Truman was President. No official explanation has ever been offered. Twice the President authorized the use of the atomic bomb on Japan in 1945 in order to end World War II.

DOGON
The Dogon people are an ethnic group in Mali, West Africa reported to have traditional astronomical knowledge about Sirius that would normally be considered impossible without the use of telescopes. They reportedly knew about the fifty year orbital period of Sirius and its companion star prior to the discovery by western astronomers. This has been the subject of controversy and speculation.

PRESIDENT OF THE UNITED STATES
Ronald Reagan, George H. W. Bush, Bill Clinton, and Barrack Obama all commented on UFO's at one time or another.

PROJECT BLUE BOOK

Was an official government report on UFO sightings that concluded that Earth was not being visited by aliens.

RICHARD NIXON
Was obsessed with UFO's and had his own personal cache of books on the subject. Legend has it that he took his close friend Jackie Gleason who was also obsessed with UFO's to an air force base to look at the alien bodies that were kept hidden there. This story has never been corroborated. All of the Moon landings by the Apollo space program occurred during the Nixon administration.

ROSWELL
Something unusual did happen in the desert of New Mexico on July 7, 1947 but it is a subject of speculation as to what occurred.

SIRIUS
Brightest star in the night sky.

TSIOLKOVSKIY CRATER
A large lunar impact crater that is located on the far side of the Moon in the southern hemisphere.

Interestingly Apollo 17 had considered the crater as a potential landing site at the suggestion of lunar module pilot and geologist Harrison Schmitt.

The plan was to use a communications satellite to communicate with Earth from the far side of the Moon. NASA nixed the idea as too costly and too dangerous.

WILKES LAND CRATER
An informal term that refers to two giant impact craters hidden beneath the ice cap of Wilkes Land, East Antarctica.

APPENDIX C
NASA SPEAKS

The general public was not particularly interested in what NASA found when they visited the Moon. Scientists at NASA remain perplexed at the findings years after the Moon landings were completed.

As NASA scientist Dr. Robin Brett once said,

"It seems much easier to explain the nonexistence of the Moon than its existence."

Here are some intriguing lessor known facts from NASA regarding the Moon.

1) They found that the soil on the Moon is older than the lunar rocks. When analyzed it was found that the soil from the Sea of Tranquility (where Apollo 11 landed) was at least one billion years older than the rocks that were found there.

This would seem to be odd since the soil should be the powdered remains of the rocks lying alongside it. Chemical analysis of the soil revealed that the lunar soil did not come from the rocks but from somewhere else.

2) Very strangely 99 percent of the Moon rocks brought back to Earth turned out upon analysis to be older than 90 percent of the oldest rocks found on Earth. The first rock that Neil Armstrong picked up after he set foot on the Moon turned out to be more than 3.6 billion years old. Other rocks were dated at 4.3, 4.5, 4.6, and even 5.3 billion years old. The oldest rocks found on Earth are about 3.7 billion years old.

These rocks all came from the area on the Moon believed to be the youngest. Based on this evidence scientists have concluded that the Moon was formed long before our earth and sun were born.

3) The three theories of the origin of the Moon all have serious problems. One was that the Moon was somehow formed alongside the Earth out of the same cosmic cloud of dust some 4.6 billion years ago. The second theory was that the Moon was the Earth's child—somehow ripped out of the Pacific basin and spun into orbit. Evidence from the Apollo missions show that the Moon and Earth vary greatly in composition so both of these theories are flawed.

Scientists now tend to lean toward a third theory—that the Moon was "captured" by the Earth's gravitational field and locked into orbit a long time ago. Opponents of this theory point to the immensely difficult celestial mechanics involved for this to happen. Accidental orbital capture of the Moon is statistically unlikely.

4) Samples brought back to Earth by both the Soviet and American space probes contain pure iron particles. These samples have not oxidized even after years on Earth. This is extremely unusual--pure iron that does not rust has not been found anywhere else.

5) The dark areas of the Moon are called "maria" or "seas" as this is what they look like from Earth—dried up sea beds. Curiously these only appear almost entirely on one side of the Moon— that facing the Earth.

Astronauts found it difficult to drill into the maria areas. The soil samples were loaded with elements like titanium, zirconium, yttrium, and beryllium. This astounded scientists because these elements require a tremendous amount of heat—approximately 4,500 degrees Fahrenheit in order to melt and fuse with surrounding rock the way it was found.

6) As part of the Apollo missions the ascent stages of the lunar module crashed on the lunar surface. Each time these caused the Moon, NASA reported, to "ring like a gong or bell". Reverberations lasted anywhere from one to up to as much as four hours. NASA has been reluctant to suggest that the Moon may actually be hollow but they cannot otherwise explain this odd fact.

7) The Moon is highly radioactive. Apollo 15 astronauts using thermal equipment determined that the heat flow near the Apennine Mountains was extremely hot. As one NASA scientist confessed, "When we saw that we said, My God this place is about to melt! The core must be very hot".

Strangely though only the surface appears to be hot—the core appears to be cold. It is unknown where all of the hot radioactive material— thorium, potassium, and uranium—came from.

8) The first few lunar missions determined that there was no water on the Moon. Yet after Apollo 15 a cloud of water vapor more than 100 square miles in size was detected on the surface. The amount of water carried by the astronauts could not possibly account for this cloud. It is postulated that the water vapor came from the interior of the Moon. Mists, clouds, and other surface changes have been reported by astronomers over the years.

9) Lunar exploration has determined that much of the surface is covered with a glass glaze — proving that the surface has been scorched by an unknown source of intense heat. Scientists have said that the surface is "paved with glass". One theory is that an intense solar flare of tremendous proportions scorched the Moon well over 30,000 years or so ago. Rather remarkably the glassy glaze is not unlike that caused by atomic weapons.

10) The Moon has little or no magnetic field — yet lunar rocks are shown to be strongly magnetized upon analysis. NASA cannot explain where this magnetic field came from.

11) Tracking data of the lunar orbiters first indicated in 1968 that there were massive concentrations of something under the surface of the circular maria that NASA calls mascons. NASA reported that the gravitational pull caused by them was so pronounced that passing spacecraft overhead dipped slightly when passing by. Scientists have decided that they are concentrations of dense, heavy matter centered under the circular maria.

The Moon from Earthside

The Moon has proven to be a mystery wrapped inside an enigma — our exploration has clearly raised many more questions than it has answered.

Recent news has revealed the potential for using radioactive lunar rocks to produce large amounts of electricity in a new generation of nuclear reactors.

NASA now believes that there is water at the south pole of the Moon and they have been searching there for it with recent probes.

The United States, China, and Russian have all announced plans to return to the lunar surface.

Veritas vos liberabit. *The truth will set you free*!

APPENDIX C
INTER GALACTIC LEGAL DISCLAIMER
DE JURE
(According to Law)
By Cassandra Hera

They are the most feared power in the Universe. Yes I am referring to lawyers and their weapon of choice — the legal system.

Your William Shakespeare got it right — "The first thing we do, let's kill all the lawyers."

On Sirius we would gladly throw the lawyers in the sea if we had one — but our water supply is precious and we do not wish to taint it. So by necessity a legal disclaimer is needed for this work.

Fear not, for legal action has already commenced as Sirius has filed long briefs in Inter Stellar Court against the Arkians for their slander. Evidence of how very serious we are concerning this matter is that we have engaged a Cercopes attorney.

Yes, you *should* quiver in fear Earthling! Our attorney is from Cercopes—where lawyers swarm like blood sucking locusts every time a pilot dings his spacecraft against another. Perhaps this obsession with litigation explains some of the behavior of those from Cercopes though we do not know for sure.

As they are so fond of saying on Cercopes *"A pound of that same merchant's flesh is thine: The court awards it, and the law doth give it."*

This line was also used by Shakespeare in the Merchant of Venice—proving he must have known Cercopes agents.

Per Inter Galactic Law all additional claims for any damages must be added to the existing litigation that is in process and must be filed on Sirius in the appropriate court of law.

Any relationship expressed or implied between *Project Blue Moon* and any persons either living or dead is purely speculative except in the cases where it is fact. Facts are facts and that is that. None of which can be proven in this case anyway since the conspiracy would not allow it.

All co-conspirators who conspired to write this novel claim diplomatic immunity ex post facto *(after the deed)*.

Apologies to the brave men and women of the Apollo program who should understand better than most the cosmic humor that has been presented herein. We would welcome you back to Danaides III anytime, we miss seeing those funny suits that you wear, but our treaty prevents such an invitation. Visit again at your own risk.

We do not believe that some musicians are agents from Arke though it is within the realm of possibility. Nonetheless readers are invited to enjoy the heavenly tunes of Judy Collins and Celine Dion. Their tunes are simply out of this world.

Jimmy Buffet is definitely worth listing to as well but as we already know Arke has disavowed any relationship with him. Strangely though, Arkians continue to search for the hidden city of Margaritaville.

Should the lost city of Margaritaville be found to be in ruins Sirius disavows any fault for any such condition therein. We too have also been unable to locate the liquid city so we could not have plundered it yet.

Readers may be enlightened by this phrase which is emblazoned on the front of the highest court on Sirius. It was also stolen by Shakespeare-- litigation is still pending.

Those that are good manners at the court are as ridiculous in the country as the behavior of the country is most mockable at the court.

--As You Like It

Patent pending on Tetron Energy Generators and on Magnetic Field Thrust engines. Any attempt to reverse engineer this technology will be met with a team of angry lawyers who will swarm your planet like crazed fans at a Justin Bieber concert.

The planet Sirius bears no responsibility for any emissions from any of the aforementioned Tetron technological achievements as our scientists have determined that Tetron is not harmful to life forms.

Exclusive rights to this book are held on all known and unknown worlds.

APPENDIX D
EARTHLY DISCLAIMER
By Joe Smith

The CIA will neither confirm nor deny the existence of Sirius, Cercopes, Earth, Danaides III, lawyers, Shakespeare, past, present or future Presidents of the United States, Dolon Ares, Adam Smith, Cassandra Hera, Claudia Quinta, Judy Collins, Celine Dion, or Jimmy Buffett or any other persons or places mentioned herein.

Should persons come across any alien artifacts, or saucer parts please forward them immediately to Wright Patterson Air Force base, c/o CIA.

Persons finding Tetron need not forward any to the CIA — we already have plenty of that. Please dispose of properly.

Please feel safe. We are watching.

ABOUT THE AUTHOR

Dolon N. Ares is a somewhat paranoid conspiracy theorist living somewhere off the grid in order to avoid detection by those who seek to find him. There are many. He keeps his location secret due to the nature of the material he presents in his controversial books. While some may call these brilliant works of fiction, Mr. Ares has made no such claim and leaves it to the reader to ascertain the facts from the fiction in his splendid works.

His latest tome *Project Blue Moon – Conspiracy In Plain Sight* will push your imagination to the max. Explore the limits of conspiracy, history, and quick wit. Read the book – learn the truth.

The publisher will neither confirm nor deny the authenticity of any information contained therein.

ACKNOWLEDGEMENT

All photography in this book is believed to be non-copyrighted material. No copyright is asserted over any of this photographic material by the author or the publisher.

In particular the author wishes to thank NASA for the privilege of using their photos and mission insignia in the making of *Project Blue Moon*.

In the event copyright infringement has occurred please contact the publisher and any unauthorized photography will be promptly removed from publication.

We leave as we came, and God willing, as we shall return, with peace and hope for all mankind.

4349435R00115

Printed in Great Britain
by Amazon.co.uk, Ltd.,
Marston Gate.